Sarah Elliot was born in Newcastle and raised in Northumberland. She was diagnosed with dyslexia at the age of ten and turned to writing her own stories as a way of keeping up her skills. She has never looked back since.

She graduated from Swansea University in 2009 with a Masters' in Creative and Media Writing and has had three plays performed by a theatrical group in Swansea. She currently works as an administrator in a care home in Newcastle and spends her free time socialising with friends, writing and taking Petal the Rottweiler for long walks.

VOLF: GOLD

Amethyst Trilogy Book 2

Sarah Elliot

Volf: Gold

Amethyst Trilogy Book 2

Vanguard Press

VANGUARD PAPERBACK

A CIP catalogue record for this title is
available from the British Library.

ISBN 9781784652272

Vanguard Press is an imprint of
Pegasus Elliot MacKenzie Publishers Ltd.
www.pegasuspublishers.com

First Published in 2017

Vanguard Press
Sheraton House Castle Park
Cambridge England

Printed and bound in Great Britain

Dedication

To my parents, as always, because I would not be here without their love, support and bragging rights

Chapter 1

Starless Night

The pungent smell of blood was going to lead the gargoyles straight to him, Dymas knew that all too well, but he could not will himself to move any further forward. He was beyond exhausted, his whole body burning with even the mere act of pushing himself unsteadily to lean more easily against the cave wall. The volf was not surprised that the air he breathed out gushed forward in large clouds of steam that slowly wound upwards and evaporated. The battle had been far too long and dangerous, especially given how close he was still to the vast manor house. He should have taken the first opportunity and fled from the grounds but the darker side of his mind doubted very much that it would have done much good. The mountains that surrounded the Manor were notorious for being virtually impassable and filled with many pitfalls that few dared to cross them.

Even the hunters, who would try on occasion to raid the vast hall, more out of a need to keep up with tradition than actually to make much headway these days, or at least that was how it appeared to the male volf, would avoid the mountains, save for the thinnest paths that led to the too well-trodden track.

Dymas cast his amber eyes around the surrounding valley, trying to discover if this natural crevice had been sought out by others before him. At first glance there was little to see, just the endless peaks of grey rocks that stretched out all around and the thick blanket of snow which coated them. In some places the drifts were enough to swallow the accursed house far below, but that was only for a fleeting moment.

As the volf stared at the grim surroundings, he thought he spotted a dark figure moving through the drifts towards him and almost began to rise despite the pain in his body, but dropped back when he realized that it was nothing more than an inquisitive robin.

Part of him wanted to snatch the bird, feast upon it, but a little robin would do nothing to still his growing need to feed upon fresh meat. The werewolf in him wanted food, overpowering his vampiric need for blood far greater than it normally would, but he knew that it was not a path to be taken lightly. It would only lead him to doing things that he would undoubtedly regret and there were already enough black marks on his soul that had sentenced him to a torturous life in hell should he die out here in the freezing snow. Though the volf knew that such a thing was not an option, that he couldn't die such a simple and pointless death like that. There were still many paths for him to tread and it would be no doubt that someone would come along to drag him back into the hell that was his life.

Excluding the one person whom he craved more than ever to see right at that moment in time. "Tyra?" Dymas whispered to the air, barely noting how the distant sounds of the few animals that lived up here had stilled in their movements. "You're supposed to be here. Where are you?"

To look upon the volf now, no one would have thought much of him. He was small, thin and weak-looking with messy white hair that needed to be trimmed and strange amber-coloured eyes that looked out at the world through a veil of sadness and disappointment. Black, wolf-like ears peaked from the top of his head, the tips of both missing as he had gotten involved in a fight he could not possibly win when he was too young to understand the consequences, and they swivelled back and forth in displeasure as he was just too cold. Dymas had barely scavenged what would pass for a decent outfit to walk through the mountains in summer, let alone the blistering freezing winter that was currently gripping the land.

There was a temptation to change, to grow the fur that would keep him warm but the beast would not be controlled tonight, Dymas knew that and he would not run the risk. Even as it clawed and howled from deep within his soul, demanding to be free, to run farther, faster than he could manage and to escape from this hell. To unleash its fearsome force upon the world and make it so that all would bow down before their great might.

Tears stung his eyes and brought Dymas back to his senses. He had worked far too hard and far too long to throw it all away on the pretence of something that he had no desire for. Still the sweet promises of oblivion did enter his mind and idly the thought was toyed with. It would be so easy to just step off the edge of the nearest cliff, to tumble down into the ravine below and have his body be smashed against the rocks to become useless, unattainable and something of interest to future explorers. To be free of this purgatory and never have to face it again.

A pure white glistening snowflake landed on his cheek and brought him back to reality. For a second he felt a childish hand touch his own and the thoughts disappeared completely from his mind as a new wave of self-awareness grabbed onto him.

What was falling from the sky wasn't normal snow, this snow was as black as the night and caused hissing singes to appear all around him. Without even stopping to consider his multiple wounds, Dymas pushed himself upright and searched fruitlessly for a place to seek better shelter in the unforgiving rock formations that were all around him. The black snow kept on falling, silent and deadly, producing long plumes of grey steam that wafted back and forth on the breeze. His sensitive nose picked up the trace of sleeping powder long before his dulled nerves could react. Mentally he cursed his ill fortune, wondering if he would have done better to follow Tyra's earlier advice of heading up the more dangerous path to meet her at the waterfall, but maybe this was a fate that he could not run away from.

He growled, desperate not to fall into the trap of such a stupid and pointless smell, but the undeniable call to sleep was going to be forthcoming very soon. The volf gritted his teeth, slumping harder against the stone mountainside and clutching at his chest as a stab of pain shot through his heart. "No… not now, not yet… I can go on… I will go on." To whom he was speaking was a mystery, but it did him a little good to hear words being spoken aloud.

Though he would have rather heard some other voice in the growing darkness, one that was caring and filled with a love that was only meant for him.

Sometimes it was hard being a lonely volf, a product of one night's mislaid passion between a broken vampire lady and a werewolf who understood the personal loss that she was suffering at the time. A part of his mind not yet completely effected by the haze of the forced sleep questioned if he was truly alone in the world, the only other like himself had been taken away from him so long ago that he had begun to think the worst. During the long lonely nights, he had been able to make himself believe that she was lying right next to him, offering support and comfort, but these days it was almost a wish that could never be fully realized.

Aware that the gargoyles hunting him were approaching his location, Dymas tried to lift his head, to stand tall and fight like he had always been taught to do, but the spell was just too powerful, the call to sleep just too tempting and the unrelenting exhaustion that had plagued his body finally managed to win out. Slumping forward, the young man knew that he was going to be in a whole lot of trouble when they got him back to the Manor, but even just the small taste of freedom had been worth every last second of pain.

Darkness swirled in his eyes before completely blocking out the light and for a long while Dymas was unaware of anything other than the blackness behind his eyes. It brought no comfort, pain or relief, just merely remained as nothing more than a darkness that brooded.

It wasn't until a red-hot ember landed on his hand that he stirred from sleep, a whimper of pain escaping his lips before he could stop it. Someone was close by, he could tell that by smell alone but he did not dare to open his eyes in case this was all an illusion, as his blasted mother was not afraid of using them given half the chance. He was aware of being in a cave, some way further up the mountain by the way the wind was whistling through the rocks and it was distinctly quiet. In fact, he could only pick up one clear scent and it put the young volf into an almost eager state of bliss.

A light shuffling of feet caught the two small ears he possessed, hidden beneath the unruly mop of white hair, and a fire burst into life as more wood was added to it, crackling merrily and bringing forth more warmth. He was surprised that anyone had been able to find dry firewood in this valley as most of it would have been absolutely useless with the heavy snows. This made him start to think that he was missing something very important about this whole situation, but he couldn't quite figure out just what.

The presence with the light feet was right next to him now, almost causing the volf to jump in surprise, but the warmth of the hand which rested lightly, caringly on top of his head was cause enough for Dymas to snap open his amber eyes without the need for the softly spoken words, "Time to arise my little lost prince."

Virtually leaping into the person's arms, though even the most erratic of doctors would have disapproved of such a thing, the boy held onto the girl as if his life depended on it. "Tyra!" He wanted to weep with relief to see the wayward spirit but instead found a frustrated anger rise up in his head causing him to lash out at her torso with his long fingernails, sending her back towards the fire. "Where the hell were you?

I waited there virtually all of the night after being attacked by…"

Tyra was once again back in his personal space, the long scratches the volf had caused simply disappearing from view as the blonde-haired spirit smiled gently and caressed his face. "You know where I was. I tried for the better part of three days to break out of that seal and, by the time I was successful, you had already gone." Her words were spoken so quietly, so softly and with such care and devotion that Dymas couldn't work out whether to be fumingly mad or overjoyously relieved that the other was there for him right now where he needed her.

The spirit was a slender young woman, with short choppy and multilayered blonde hair and a complexion that always reminded him of ash that somehow managed to appear healthy. Her build wasn't quite athletic but it wasn't skinny either, it was sort of in-between and had been styled to appeal only to him alone. Tyra wasn't meant to do such things but she had long ago declared her uttermost resolve to him and always broke the rules. Just in order to please him in any way that she could.

Latching onto her again, though mentally scolding himself for nearly collapsing into a sodden wreck of tears, the volf clung to the love of his life even as he lightly battered at her chest with his fists. "Why didn't you come straight to me? You've done it before! Why did you leave me like that?"

"I didn't," replied the spirit, twisting the young man back a little before raising his head, her fingers feeling soft and inviting whilst her eyes sparkled with a million stars. They were a deep electric shimmering blue, like an exploding star Dymas noted. "You know that I would not do such a thing to you." A mischievous smile crossed her features, exposing her slightly sharp teeth, "But when there are nearly two score of gargoyles out after the runaway, taking care of them is no easy task." Smiling gently, she pressed her body closer to the boy, bridging the gaps between their lips and caressing his body with her hands expertly.

A startled gasp escaped Dymas, which Tyra used to her full advantage to slip her tongue into his mouth and start a heated, needful make-out session with her prince whom she had missed so much. It didn't take Dymas long to respond, his hands gliding over the spirit's barely covered form feeling the soft, smooth skin that tingled under his fingertips.

Suddenly he stopped, pulling back with a hurt expression towards the female spirit, "This is a dream, isn't it? You're creating a place where we can be together, aren't you?"

The spirit tutted in annoyance before pouting and giving a nod though she did not seem happy about it at all. "I was hoping that you wouldn't notice till afterwards but…" With a shrug, Tyra moved to reclaim the other's lips, happy to feel him respond even though he now knew the truth of the situation.

Finally, they pulled apart and Tyra sighed. "One of these days I will work out how to confuse you enough with dreams to get what we both want," she chuckled lightly, running a hand down the volf's chest and receiving a sad smile in return.

"I would rather have you in the flesh," Dymas smirked, blushing a light tinge of red before resting his hand on the side of Tyra's face, "What in the world would I do without you by my side?"

Closing her eyes, Tyra leaned back down for another kiss, gently lowering the boy to the floor, "Probably give into despair. I must leave now; you are too close. I will try to find a way out, I promise you," a reflective pause consumed her for a second, "How did you work it out anyway? I thought that I had everything covered?"

Dymas smiled and sneakily ran his hand over the exquisite flesh. "You know full well that smooth skin only belongs on one creature in this entire world and right now she is far away from here and safe."

"I wouldn't count overly much on that," Tyra murmured but before she could explain further, the dream world shattered in a flurry of black and gold.

A stinging sensation ran through his cheek, breaking through the haze of clogged-up thoughts but not enough to reveal anything coherent to Dymas. A second slap, much harder and delivered from a hand covered in a very heavy metal, brought the dark and snowy world into focus as well as the vile scum that was once again snarling into his face with broken, yellowed teeth.

"He ain't dead," said the owner, a vile man who had been rightfully named Brutus when he was born, "though I bet he will wish he was by the time they're finished with him." Dymas noted that unlike the rest of the gargoyles, who were a motley bunch of pebble creatures that his mother created from ancient magic because they were far quicker to make in comparison to fully fledged gargoyles and did not come with the usual problems of developing a personality beyond much more of a loyal dog that did not know it was doing, Brutus could vaguely pass for being human. If he wasn't the colour of dark stone with a series of pigeon feathers that almost made him appear to have hair. He still had strength about him that rivalled many humans however and the volf thought it was best not to push the matter too much.

Instead Dymas coughed a little, sending a splatter of blood onto the one who was carrying him despite the gag biting at the edge of his lips, and for a moment he felt his stomach twist. He was definitely reaching the frenzy stage and needed to satisfy the blood lust soon but with his hands, feet and mouth bound heavily he knew that there were next to no chance. Still he struggled a little, trying to get away even though he knew that they were at the gates to the place he least wanted to be and, once they were closed, there would be no escape from the Manor of Cresta Du Winter.

Chapter 2

Preparation for the Ritual

The Manor was a grand building, a rather modest – by vampire standards – fifteen-bedroom house with several libraries, a grand ball room and an almost undetectable series of underground rooms with a single spiralling staircase that led down to them. They were dark and harboured only a little light, which the volf was both glad of and desperate to avoid as with long intersecting tunnels connecting the darkened rooms beneath the Manor it made navigation complicated even for the seasoned guard.

He knew that he would be soon destined to go back into those horrible rooms but he wished it weren't so. In fact, he had wished more than a thousand times that he had not survived the first few ill-fated hours of his life, or even if he did have to come into existence then he would have preferred to be either a fully-fledged werewolf or even better a vampire. Maybe then his mother wouldn't be so evil towards him and his sister. Though an ironic twist of a smile appeared on his face at that thought, Cresta Du Winter would have been evil towards them regardless of what they actually were. Even her most favoured son at one time had not been able to escape her wrath when she was brought to full anger, so they would have been no different.

Dropped onto the snowy ground unexpectedly in the large courtyard that had once held a beautiful fountain that was now a choked mockery of its former self, Dymas was thankful for the gag that effectively did its job and kept him from whimpering aloud as his knees and elbows smarted against the hard stone under the snow. Unbidden, the amber eyes drifted upwards to see the absolutely furious beauty that was the Northern Vampire Lady.

Standing at only five foot three, most would not have been perplexed by her initial appearance save for those who stared into the emerald green eyes. Whilst she looked on the surface like an enviously beautiful and extremely well preserved forty-five-year-old her eyes spoke of an age of virtually uncontrolled anger, hatred and a longing for a power that was far greater than any creature in the world should have wished for. Her size seemed to magnify itself, especially with the addition of the golden blonde hair that swept majestically back from her face and down her back. Tonight it was swept up high to match the high collar of her dark red dress and a few carefully placed kiss curls cascaded down to make her appear just as beautiful as any high lady of the realm should look. Her lips were set in a tight line, however, which showed her displeasure at having to deal with him again, though the rest of her face appeared quite calm and relaxed and her posture suggested that she was merely there for formalities.

However, Dymas wasn't stupid; he knew only too well what she was capable of and right now every last ounce of anger was going to be directed at himself. "So, the runaway returns?" it was a rhetoric question of course, since not even Dymas had an answer to give, seeing that Brutus had used sleeping powder to bring him back to the Manor. "Not even the threat of his lover's life on the line appears to be enough to keep him line. What am I to do with a nearly worthless whelp like you?"

A strangled gasp of surprise was ripped out of the boy's throat when the gag was forcibly ripped off; the corner of his mouth caught and ruptured just enough to cause a trickle of blood to roll down his chin and onto his tongue. "You can't kill Tyra!" he shouted, spitting at the woman's feet. "Just like you can't kill me!"

Cresta stepped towards her illegitimate son and struck him harshly on each cheek, adding to the pain that was still lingering from Brutus's previous slap. She leaned down, face to face with a sneer as her fingers wrapped themselves around his white hair to prevent him from looking away, "That is where you are completely wrong. I can kill that simpering little cow and you, with just the merest of mere thoughts." One of her long, red-painted fingernails ran along his throat and it was so hard to not automatically swallow in fear. "But I have a far greater need for you, my bastard son, so your blood will not be spilled further. Unless you give me a good reason to end your existence and take away everything that is important to you. Do not hold to the hope in your heart that the silver one can help you… she is in my keeping now and soon I will have everything that I need."

"Ekata?" Dymas breathed, instinctively reaching out his senses to find his twin sister but relieved when no response was received, "She is not here. You lie bitch." Another grimace was drawn forth as his mother gently stroked his left ear with her long fingernails, almost as if she cared about him.

"Extend your call to beyond the mountains," was the whispered command and, unable to resist such words though he did not know quite as to why, Dymas did as he was bidden. The range of the call was far greater than he had ever tried before and sent spasms of pain throughout his whole body, but a cry of sheer disbelief steadily built up.

He saw the plain-looking wagon, with guards and a few followers, heading down the long winding road that led through the lower parts of the mountains. He saw the figure of Siren, seated with the reins of the horses, looking content with herself and humming in that dark style of hers whenever she knew that death was close beside her. Mephistopheles strangely was not in view, though presumably he was in one of the large crates on the wagon.

Dymas knew automatically which one contained his sister; he even accidentally dived straight down below the wooden top to see her slumbering face. For a second he lost all sense of reality and screamed her name aloud, seeing her open her identical amber eyes in response, but the very next second he was ripped back to the snow-covered world.

A tiny blast of wind, summoned up either by him or from being pulled back too unexpectedly it was hard to say, fluttered around his person but was effective enough to push Cresta away from his body by a few small steps.

"Why?" Dymas screamed, anger seething through him as he tried to pick himself up despite still being bound, and half stumbled back to the unforgiving floor. "Why do you do this to us? What did we ever do?" He did not notice the golden swirls on his bruised and battered body that began to glow softly as he focused on the insane woman who was in front of him, but she gave no indication of noticing them either.

"You were born," was the answer, delivered with an almost playful little smirk, and it was the only answer that he knew he would ever receive from the mad woman who had given birth to him before she turned away. Cresta appeared to be unconcerned about the volf's attempts to lash out, as really they only resulted in causing more injuries to Dymas himself and started heading back to the mansion, "Get that rat cleaned up and to the Worshiper, we do not have much time to waste on such trivial matters."

Barely able to struggle, Dymas snarled in her direction as he was hauled up from the ground by the guards, determined that the wetness of his eyes was to do with his anger and were not, under any circumstances, tears. He could have shouted a thousand and one curses and insults towards the woman but they would have just fallen on deaf ears. His head slumped, he had no idea who the Worshiper was but already he knew that he wouldn't like what was to come.

He barely registered that he was led down into the depths of the underground corridors, until his eyes fell on a glistening pool, lined with grey marble and surrounded by women who were preparing scented oils. It was a place that he completely detested and shivers ran down his spine.

If there was one thing in the world that Dymas didn't like – other than being deprived of his faithful lover, of course – it was getting a bath. Not that he didn't mind water, that was fine and soap to a certain extreme as well, but just being in the bath with a bunch of mauled and maimed servants did not appeal to him in the slightest. Especially considering the fact that most of the time the bath was not for the sole purpose of cleaning his body, it was used to prepare him for whatever mad plan Cresta had come up with in order to steal forth the powers that apparently lay dormant within his body. So far, 277 different priests, prophets, warmongers, soothsayers and other related persons had tried to call forth this apparent dormant energy and, out of that number, only two had ever got any real results.

The first one had been officially recorded as the first bloodletting Dymas ever did without the guiding hand of an elder sibling who actually loved him for who he was, and he couldn't remember much of what had happened to the second one. Though from what little evidence remained of the person in question, it was clear that some form of deadly battle had taken place. But not even Tyra would tell him the full specifics of that night, another thought to worry him in the bitter darkness whenever he was left completely alone for a short stretch of time.

Brutus and his men had no troubles removing the ragged clothes from Dymas's form, it was a way to save time and it allowed the leader to get a grip on the volf's body. Whilst Dymas had always fought off this attention and made his opinion very clear on the matter, Brutus kept on stealing what he could and both knew that if the opportunity ever presented itself, then the leader would take the boy willingly or not.

Thankfully two servants came to snatch him away from the gargoyles and virtually threw Dymas into the quite frankly stunning marble pool that was to serve as his bath. Dymas tried ineffectually to fight against the sudden appearance of two badly disfigured servants who knew nothing of their twisted fate. They were ensnared into the power of Cresta, completely convinced that they were beautiful immortal beings who would stand alongside their mistress through all levels of hell. In reality they were nothing more than lingering husks that had been beaten, misshapen and destroyed into becoming vile, grotesque forms of humanity that followed orders like a pack of hungry dogs. These two were well known to him, Philipson and Thorez, two of the eldest creations and twisted creatures who now looked more like gnarled trees than two once-handsome young men.

The problem with these two was, whilst they looked quite hideous and easy to break, they were unnaturally strong and could easily withstand most of the things that they were tasked with. If truth be told, Cresta Du Winter favoured them the most out of her creations because they were almost near perfection in terms of the loyalty that she demanded from her subjects. So when Dymas tried to escape from the water, their long crooked fingers latched firmly onto his twig-like arms and effortlessly dragged him into the very centre of the bath.

"Let me go!" he started to scream before finding himself forced underwater and held for a few terrible seconds.

Instincts kicked in and he thrashed about in desperation to breath, before he was hauled out, coughing and spluttering and then forcibly thrown back under the water. However instead of being the clear crystal it had been before, it was clogged with the mud, blood, twigs and other unsavoury substances which had previously been stuck to his skin and hair. The filthy water ran up his nose and dived into his mouth, chasing after the small pockets of air that still resided deep within his lungs. Once again he was thrashing about but this time the gnarled monstrosities did not pull him free after a few seconds. Part of his brain that was not succumbing to complete and total panic, realized that they were deliberately trying to drown him and the sudden knowledge fired through his brain like a lightning bolt.

Just able to get his feet on the bottom of the bath, Dymas kicked out sharply against the floor to launch himself back up and out of the water. However, before he could break the surface, both of the servants were suddenly underwater with him, pulling him down to the bottom of the pool, seemingly unconcerned by the notion of a watery grave. The volf struggled, trying desperately to break free but his field of vision began to narrow at an alarming rate and a voice, tiny and almost impossible to hear, whispered gently in the back of his mind, *it would be good to just give up. Then all the pain would stop and I would be free.*

Slowly his movements stilled, becoming less desperate and more just allowing the water to do what it felt like with him. It would be so easy to go like this, everyone else could be blamed and he would be free of all of his mother's mad ravings. However, another voice, stronger and full of deep baritones overpowered the tiny whisper with a cry of *YOU CANNOT GIVE UP! BOTH YOUR LIVES DEPEND ON THE OTHER! WAKE UP!*

A fiery red light suddenly surrounded him and the water boiled to the point where it blistered his skin red raw. Dymas was convinced that he was going to be burnt alive.

But the next second, Dymas found himself clawing his way out of the side of the pool, coughing up as much water as he possibly could do whilst taking in all the available oxygen in the room. His vision was still hazy but at some level he was aware that the servants had released him and were silently raising themselves out of the water. However, they bore the signs of having been viciously burned by something, though he could not work out what until he happened to glance down at his arms where they had been holding him.

The ever-present gold lines, thin with the appearance of having been etched onto his pale skin, shimmered darkly back at him. The gold was a much deeper colour than it normally was, which worried him far more than it should do.

"Well, well, well," said a voice and Dymas swiftly turned to see the man he could only presume to be the Worshiper. "It appears that the child cannot die unless the other presence is also weakened. A handy tip for our future work, I do believe." The man couldn't have been more than forty nor younger that twenty-five but it was extremely hard to tell. His face was gaunt, more like skin stretched across bone with dark sunken patches and glimmering pure white eyes. The male volf didn't doubt for a second that he was blind; clearly the Worshiper had seen everything that had gone on just now so they would be no mistakes this time around.

A slight strain of fear tugged at his heart, but it was quenched out by the anger of what the man in the grey robes had said. "You will not touch her, I will see to it myself," he said in warning, his amber eyes shimmering dangerously in a threat which the Worshiper simply laughed at before rising.

He was a good deal taller than was to be expected but his mass was craftily hidden underneath a series of mismatched pieces of gauze fabric that gave the impression of a dark-coloured, wraith-like bird. Looking down at Dymas he snorted, “I don’t doubt such a thing from such a person as you, little wet volf, but her fate will always rest in your hands and if you do not do your duty at the right moment then all will fade into darkness,” glancing up at the servants he scowled, “Take him to the preparation rooms and make him decent. If he is to meet with the Gods of Death, he should at least look less like the rat that he is.”

Staring at the man in some amount of confusion, Dymas barely noticed the two servants wrap their fingers around his arms once again and drag him out of the water. His head swam with a thousand and one thoughts, trying to work out which Gods of Death he actually meant. If there was one thing that he had learned in this bitter existence, it was the fact that Death had many faces, but they all led to one result.

“Scrub him clean,” Thorez’s voice broke him out of the string of constantly swirling thoughts, “and make sure he is fully prepared for the Worshiper.”

Physically jumping back in fright from the figure that was approaching him now, the volf wished nothing more than to remain in the vile hands of the two monsters that currently had him.

“We will ensure that he is made to be a thing of almost perfection,” said the currently speaking haricord, a vile amalgamation of a fallen angel and a resurrected demon, sprinkled with just enough venom of Frey folk to make them virtually uncontrollable beasts who lusted after men’s souls to feast upon for all eternity. “For one day he will be our Master and we cannot have him trapped in such an ugly skin.”

"Take a look in the mirror, urchin," Dymas spat, ripping his arm away from Philipson who had not as of yet released him. "At least I have a face that's my own."

The speaker, in most men's eyes, would have appeared to be enchantingly beautiful. Similar to one of those maidens who stepped straight out of a storybook with snow-white skin, blood-red lips and dark onyx hair and an air of innocence about her that was almost sickening to the core. Had Dymas not been in love with Tyra he would have possibly fallen under her spell, as the glamour of the haricord was more addictive than their much lesser cousins, the harpies.

The haricord just chuckled before latching one of her spidery long fingers onto his arm, eliciting a hiss of pain from Dymas, "The boy will be ready by nightfall. Me and my sisters shall see to it."

Before an argument could form on his lips, the volf found himself quite literally ripped away from the two maimed servants and into the preparation chambers, which he hated at least a thousand times more than ever having a bath. With speed and strength that he could only hope to match one day, the haricords dragged him onto a metal circle to which his feet were attached on one side and his wrists were dragged up above his head, before being locked just as firmly as they always were.

Dymas tried not notice the various young haricords as they slithered and slid around his suspended form, removing the rags of dead skin from his body, teasing the old wounds with their fingers and lips to elicit a fresher blood flow until they were chased off by the elder sisters. Water cascaded over his now naked form, warm and filled with soap that made the cuts smart over his entire body, no matter how much he tried to think of other things. The sisters began chanting, a strange noise that twisted his heart in pain, drew forth whimpers and an even greater longing to be out of this place.

Two of the sisters, one looking like a possessed doll, the other similar to that of a squashed spider stood either side of his head and began cleaning all of the mess out of his ragged hair. The soap got inside his two, very small and hidden wolf-like ears and in irritation he flicked them back and forth to get rid of the bubbles, but this only enticed the strange beings to do it more frequently.

For a while the volf made himself unaware of what they were doing, focusing his body into an almost unconscious state that it made this whole experience easier to deal with. He didn't notice that his hands were unchained nor his feet had the exact same thing done to them as well, but Dymas was jolted by a sudden wave of nausea that threatened to send him down to his knees. For a second he was confused by it but then felt the sharpness of a tooth against his lower lip. The Hunger was almost upon him and he didn't want to think of the victim he would be forced to feed upon in order to remain in this disgusting form of life that he had been granted. "Blood," he whispered towards the haricords, hoping uselessly that they would give him something that would appease his appetite.

Instead they giggled, grabbed his hair and dragged him into an upright standing position to dress him as had been requested by the Worshiper. It was pretty much the standard affair, a plain black pair of trousers with no belt and two ribbons around his wrists to stop him biting at the skin. Strangely a few new additions were made to the standard attire, his hair was brushed back into a tight ponytail, which exposed his ears far more than they usually would, and a top, coloured like the blackest of night and made out of fine silk, was placed on his shoulders.

Frowning, the boy went to ask questions but felt himself sway and found himself in a long, square and sparsely decorated room that he knew was at the opposite end of the mansion to where he had just been. His amber eyes darted around in fright and panic before a light tapping noise caught his attention. There, standing by itself on an old wooden table, was an ancient looking glass jar where a familiar-looking figure was attempting to break out.

Dymas virtually charged at the jar, wrapping his fingers around it despite the burning sensation it caused, "Tyra!" he could have wept if he were not so furious, half-terrified out of his mind and so relieved to find the one person whom he loved beyond the bounds of family ties. "What did she do to you?"

The spirit stared helplessly at the volf from inside the glass prison, knowing that it would be impossible to speak a word to the other, despite her need to just gather up the gorgeously handsome boy in front of her and never let him go ever again. Lightly she shook his head, "Dymas, run. Get out of here whilst you still can."

The volf stared at the jar, wondering what spells were on it in order to keep Tyra trapped and barely registered the presence of another in the room until a hand landed firmly on the back of his neck and sharply tugged him away. The jar clattered from Dymas's grasp, and it rolled around in a circle, causing Tyra to stumble but still try to reach him through the glass. It didn't shatter like Dymas had hoped it would.

"The Prince must come along," said the Worshiper, his voice filled with a dreadful seriousness; "the preparations must be complete within the next six days."

"What are you driveling about now, old man?" Dymas managed to choke out as he was hauled away effortlessly by the Worshiper. "What's so special about the next six days?"

A smile, cold and crooked a little on the left, crossed the bear-like man's face. "You turn eighteen."

A cold sense of dread passed through Dymas. His eighteenth birthday was rumored to be the time when either the Golden Prince or the Black King would arise to take the world under his protective gaze or destroy it beneath his mighty shield. It couldn't be 29th February in six days, it just couldn't be. But part of him knew all too well that the day was dawning and now it was clear why his mother's interest in them had perked up somewhat.

"Please, someone help us," he murmured slightly as he was thrown out of the room and into the thorn garden by the Worshiper. Tyra glowered behind her glass prison, bashing her fist so hard against the glass in frustration that a tiny crack began to appear but, at that moment in time, the spirit didn't notice it.

Chapter 3

Taking a Beating

"You incompetent fool!" The voice cut sharply through the grand entrance hall, echoing back off the various statues and ornaments which were gaudily placed to give the illusion of grandeur. "I give you one mere task to perform and as usual you fail dismally at it. Why I even bother with you Akira is a mystery even to myself!"

The young man on the floor barely looked up from his kneeling position in front of Cresta; he was more than used to receiving these sorts of lectures. It would never matter how well he did on any task that he was assigned to, Akira was always going to be called a fool, useless and pathetic because he could never match up to his eldest brother Mephistopheles. The pain from realizing that had faded over the years, but sometimes still just stung a little.

Gently he sighed, though so softly as not to be detected. "It was not me that failed, mother, the guard of honour did not take into account that the spirit would be guarding the—"

"You should have told them!" shrieked Cresta, swirling about the floor in her dress of green and blue which made her look a little like a sea urchin in Akira's mind, but he was smart enough to not voice that comment in the slightest. Vanity was a dangerous trait to have and his mother had plenty of it to go around for every last member of their family. Not that he was afflicted with such a thing, out of all of his siblings, even those who shared his father but not his mother, he was the plainest and ordinary looking. Standing at five foot eight with brown hair and pale brown eyes he was average in everything. All the rest got the lion's share of the beauty and that extra supernatural allure that characterized most vampires, whereas he appeared to be the cast-off from some human relationship.

Aware that Cresta was closer now, Akira carefully pulled himself up off the floor and shook his head, "Mother, I told them everything that they needed to know. You were there next to me when I gave the orders."

The lithe woman was suddenly staring at him with her blazing emerald-green eyes, her fangs descended in a raging fury which immediately put the younger vampire on guard. "So now you blame me for your failure, you worthless imp!" Fast as lightning, her fist collided with the side of his face, sending him into a tumbling spin that was only brought to an abrupt stop from years of practice since he had, at one time, been the favoured punchbag of this highly dangerous lady. "I should send you to the Elders and force them to make you a true vampire instead of the pathetic monster who sits at my feet and begs for the beating to stop! You are no vampire, Akira, you are a non-existent puppet with no will or soul of your own!" Her tirade continued; "I will destroy you once and for all!"

Bracing himself for the flurry of impacts that he knew was coming, Akira found himself wishing that maybe this time she really would destroy him. It would be a welcome relief from the constant disappointment that she gave him for not being like his elder brothers and maybe he would be able to finally be reborn as someone stronger. It was only when the side of his head cracked against a marble step, sending a spray of blood out in a near perfect circle, that the young vampire even registered the fact that he was being repeatedly struck.

"Mother, stop it!" he yelled as some inner instinct flared inside him, the need to survive for a reason that he could no longer remember and he lashed out at the woman, catching her cheek with the back of his fingers just hard enough to turn her face away but not enough to do any damage. The pain kicked in, whatever trance-like state he had put himself into shattering into thin shards of glass that rippled throughout his body but no sound would he allow himself to make, excluding the heavy panting which ran ragged with the bitter taste of blood.

For a few long, heavy seconds everything was silent and then Cresta turned back to her son with a look of absolute horror on her face, "Akira?" she asked, kneeling down next to him, her voice so soft, gentle and worried that he felt his heart was being torn apart by a pack of wild dogs, "Who did this to you? Who hurt my baby boy?"

A part of his mind screamed at her, tried to pull away from that beautiful softness which he craved above all other things, but Akira's body and mind were caught up in just far too much pain to bring himself to deny this one moment's vice. Her hands were gentle upon his face, so caring and motherly that he closed his eyes in shame for having ever wanting to leave her side. Tears spilled silently from the closed lids and painfully he pulled her into a rough, one-armed hug as the other was lying broken at his side. "It doesn't matter," he managed to croak out, "not in the slightest."

"I will kill them," Cresta said, hugging tightly into the boy's side. "I will kill all of them that hurt you and your siblings. No one hurts what is mine and gets away with it."

For a second Akira pondered the notion that his mother truly was insane or suffering from schizophrenia but brushed it from his mind. Right now he could only do what he could do for her and if that meant getting beaten up in order to rediscover who she was underneath all of the hatred, lies and deceit that she had built up over the years, then he would take it. "I will heal soon," he whispered, gulping down a feeling of nausea which threatened to overflow from his gut, as there was nothing worse than throwing up on the woman you were trying to calm down.

Cresta shifted, "If only your brother was here, he would sort this mess out."

"He is here," Akira replied, not understanding her words.

"No he is not. There is something that looks like him but it is not him," Cresta replied, shuddering and nestling a little closer, "I should have never driven him away. All he ever did was fill that place in the family that was gone… I drove him away when I should have kept him so close. Maybe I would have been a better mother to you and Siren, maybe I would be a better mother to those two children who I now have no choice but to destroy… maybe I wouldn't have even discovered their purpose in the world if he had just…"

Akira choked on some disgusting congealed blood which broke the concentration of the woman who rose a little to check on her youngest vampire son. He was dismayed to see the light of innocence fading and fierce deadly beauty return to her eyes, realizing that he was once again looking upon the face of the woman who his father had married and Mephistopheles had grown up with. The face he had only seen briefly in his early childhood before the tragic events which led her to changing into a monster without any morals or goals.

"My baby boy, I'll get you some help," she said, rising and heading away.

Akira tried to reach out to her, to keep her by his side for a little longer but was already aware that it was far too late. Cresta had barely gone five paces before she slowed and her stance changed. Instead of being the soft, caring woman she had been mere seconds before, she was now a distinguished and devastatingly beautiful demon who bore only contempt for the world.

Glancing back over her shoulder, she frowned at Akira as though she had no clue as to what had just occurred between them before looking down to her blood-soaked hands and shrugging her shoulder.

"You!" she said, snapping her fingers at a maimed fallen angel servant. "Fetch some blood for that worthless fool and get this place cleaned up. If he needs extra attention take him to see the healer. I'm so disappointed in your Akira; I would have thought you would have come back from that battle with only minor wounds."

There was no point in correcting the woman in regards to the situation but Akira was still reeling from the brief moment of having his true mother back who genuinely cared for him. Being rejected for being weak in comparison to a brother was hard enough but knowing that somewhere, deep down inside the same dangerous woman was a soft, gentle soul virtually shattered the young man. Gently he pushed himself up, trying to focus his vision but finding it hazy until the servant returned with the blood.

Snatching the glass, he greedily drank his fill and thrust it back towards the angel, "More, bring the whole damn bottle."

Without making a sound, the twisted angel nodded and headed away once again whilst Akira painfully picked himself up with the intention of leaving the room and his mother to her own vices. Instead however he couldn't help but be drawn back towards her as a large black crow called nosily as it landed on a nearby window sill. Cresta was reading a message that had just been delivered, her hay-coloured hair brushing back and forth in the wind from the open window.

Slowly she turned, "They have reached the southern mountain path. In two days they will be back here with their cargo."

Akira blinked, he was well aware that they had captured the missing volf but he had thought that Mephistopheles would not take the southern path. It was the easier of the two in most circumstances, especially during the harsh winters, but there were many devastating memories along that path for the older vampire which constantly made him try to avoid it. "That doesn't seem like him," he thought aloud, eyes only slightly widening in fear when he realized what he had done not a second later.

Staring at him inquisitively, Cresta silently asked the question which automatically compelled him to answer, "Mephistopheles normally avoids the southern path at all costs. From what little I gathered something happened on that road to him and Siren that made him fearful to go down there unless all other routes were cut off. The snow is not bad enough to have cut off the northern or the lake trails and neither route are longer than the one he takes. It just seems out of place for him."

The vampire lady paused to think over this statement before smiling, "I forgot how insightful you can be Akira. You are right that path is seldom the route that he would take. Which means that he is not in control of himself at the moment."

"What do you mean, Mother?" Akira couldn't help but ask.

For a few seconds he thought that he wasn't going to get his answer and merrily distracted himself when the servant turned up with the blood he had asked for. Rudely he grabbed the bottle and went to drink from it, but found Cresta's hand resting on top.

"Why don't you take one of the blood dolls?" she said. "They will give you more strength back than drinking it like that."

Akira sighed. "The usual offerings are being held up by the snows so there's only a couple left. It makes no difference to me, cold or warm it's all the same. But what did you mean about Mephistopheles not being in control of himself?"

There was a tightening of the other's lips for a few seconds before she sighed, "Not entirely, I think that he just forgot the one simple rule when stealing another's life from them."

"Stealing another's…" Akira was forced to pause by the pounding in his head that for a second made him reel sideways but he was thankfully able to catch himself before he did any further damage to himself or the walls.

Cresta appeared not to have noticed and instead stared out across the dark valley, "When one takes someone's name, power and life they must ensure to destroy the original completely else eventually the perpetrator will be caught. He may think that I have forgotten all about my first son but I still remember. Not that it matters, his actions are predictable and by the time he realizes that he is merely a puppet in this game it will be far too late for him."

The smile that accompanied the statement made Akira's skin crawl, but he did not let it bother him overly much for now as he thought slowly over the woman's words. Something that was a little hard after the beating that had just been delivered to him.

The green eyes turned to him, "Have you ever thought about what you would do if you could take someone's place Akira? What you would change for your own satisfaction?"

Not feeling up to replying, Akira took a long healthy swig from the bottle of fresh blood before offering it to his mother. He could feel his broken bones knitting themselves back together, an uncomfortable sensation but one that he was used to. Cresta smiled up at him, just shaking her head before she walked past him to deal with other matters. Strangely she gave him no orders which left him a little at a loss as to what to do but he brushed it off as being nothing more than a brief saving grace that had been extended to him.

He waited until the vampire woman was gone before slumping to the ground once again and letting out a string of curses as he tried desperately to think straight. He had known that things in the Manor were not good and that if he was not careful then he could not achieve his goals, but the cold shudder that roamed his body made him just ever more worried than before.

The crow cawed at him expectantly, beak snapping and Akira glared at it, "I know," he hissed, sneering a little. "Just a few more days and then everything will be set in motion. I just have to keep on going… have to be here, by her side so that she doesn't suspect."

The crow tilted its head, almost as if in understanding and Akira chuckled towards it, raising the bottle to his lips to take a deeper drink. "The ritual won't work," he whispered to the darkness. "I'll make sure of it. I know where everything is and I'll make sure that the twins are saved. They deserve it, after what she's put them through."

Once again there came a loud caw and the crow was off the ledge, circling back to wherever it had come from and Akira smiled as he finally relaxed against the wall and let his eyes close. He may be nothing to his mother but he was surely useful to someone else in the world and that lifted his spirits no end.

Chapter 4

Prison of Ice

Jolting awake, Tyra at first couldn't quite work out where she was or why everything was moving so quickly. Trying to stand proved to be fruitless as she just tumbled back to the floor, swaying back and forth like she was a marble caught inside a jar. A momentary pause allowed her to confirm that she was actually bouncing around the jar which held her prisoner.

She felt the jar shudder to a stop, a constant trembling replacing the jerky movements and Tyra wished not for the first time that she could just break out to cause havoc and destruction. There was an exchange going on above her, a gruff-sounding voice which could have only belonged to a guard demanding to know something whilst a terrified but sweet voice tried to explain. However, the walls of the jar were covered with yellow paper and she could not see outside, which was frustrating.

A whimper that was all too familiar reached her ears and the spirit blinked her blue eyes. "Isa?" she whispered, wondering just what the broken half-angel was doing in this sort of situation before finding herself roughly jerked to the side as the jar was effortlessly ripped from the servant's fingers.

Twisting back onto her feet hurriedly, Tyra snarled at the face staring back at her through the glass as the paper fell away. It was a face that even the most loving mother would have trouble loving as it was all sharp angles, with pock-marked scabs and a constant leer that would make the local master of entertainments feel disgusted. The spirit had learned long ago it was pointless to learn the names of these heathens; they were hired mercenaries who got paid a lot of money to obey Brutus and the vampire lady without question. They went by whatever name sounded good at the time and their only good trait was the fact that they emitted a smell so vile and gross that any creature with half a nose could tell when they were coming from half a mile away. "Looks like your little friend could use a dip in the water," the scabby-faced man laughed. "You shouldn't have tried to…"

The last words of the sentence faded in a rather surprised sounding squawk as a sudden eruption of blood splattered across the creature's face as a hundred different blisters, scabs, boils, spots and unattended scratches burst forth with fresh gusto. The mercenary, upon finally realizing what had just happened, let out a yell and dropped the jar which gave Isa the chance to grab it and run.

Two solid minutes of running later and they could still hear the man shrieking despite having been brought up never to do such a thing. Tyra was still reeling from the fact that the curse she had thrown in hasty anger had actually managed to get through to do its damage when, for the second time, there was a blinding flash and the sound of a voice saying, "Jumerkra!"

Hitting the floor hard, Tyra felt herself sink a good two or three inches into the stone before she was able to focus.

Hauling herself upright, the blonde-haired spirit took several long deep breaths of air to ground herself in this plain of reality before solidifying her body completely. Turning she stared at the broken half-angel, feeling the weight of sorrows fall onto the boy who simply shook his head in response. "I may not be with him but my heart will forever be his," Isa sighed, declining the unspoken offer of help. His small body was wrecked to a far greater degree than most of the servants, it was twisted and contorted, like he had been pulled apart and fitted back together by an armature causing him to walk with an odd, stooping gait that was pitiful to behold. However, despite the ugly outlook, it was impossible to call the man anything but wonderful as his soft, washed-out summer eyes and just remaining gentle features spoke of a time when he had not been like this.

Even his broken wings, which were the colour of funeral shrouds, were impossible to miss. "At least let me pay you back for all you have done," Tyra said, shifting closer as if to reach out to the boy only to have her hand knocked away with a sullen shake of the head.

"He needs you more than me right now." The sadness in Isa's smile was heartbreaking. "Go to him, before your time runs out. I will more than likely *entertain* the guards for a little while. Go… now."

Rising slowly, the spirit sighed before bowing low to the boy and heading quickly down the only available path. She pretended to not notice that the stones of the corridor began to mould and shape themselves to form a wall behind her, which had never been there in the first place. She heard the fatalistic cry as the guards caught up with Isa, but knew that turning back would be a complete waste of time as there was nothing she could do for the fallen angel.

Pausing as she reached the end of the passageway, the spirit glanced up at the darkening sky, aware that her breath was steaming heavily in front of her but not caring for such things, feeling a storm coming on. How was it possible for rain to fall in the middle of winter when it should have frozen into slithers of ice or soft white snow? She didn't know the answer but she knew that she would have to move quickly if she wanted to help Dymas out in any way tonight.

Bracing herself for feeling a completely different kind of cold in comparison to most other creatures in this realm, Tyra headed out into what could only be described as an overgrown thorn garden. At one time it had been a beautiful stretch of many coloured roses that were bewitched to grow in the night so that the family could sit and enjoy them. Now however all of the fine petals had long since wilted away to shrivelled, blackened stumps and only the cruel, sharp and wicked thorns remained, scuttling through the pathways and wrapping themselves fiercely around anything that happened to be there.

Stumbling with an annoyed growl, the spirit righted herself in surprise when she found the branches retreating from her before slowly turning around. Almost immediately she felt a wave of harsh nausea and a desperate urge to run struck deep within her mind, but the spirit brushed it off before marching forward. Evil had come to live in this place and it never liked to be disturbed by her presence, preferring to claw away at a mind it could actively deal with.

There was a pond that was oval in shape, with what at one time had been a nice little marble white trim around the circumference but it was now covered in grime and choking vines. Tyra made a beeline straight for it as instead of an oozing, oily-like surface that rippled with whatever creature was being forced to die a very long, sullen death, there was a sheet of pure black ice lying over the top of the water. Faint images, greyish-brown in colour, swarmed just underneath and, sitting in the centre, was a vile-looking goblin that was guarding the entrance.

Tyra didn't even need to hear the half-choked, muffled screams nor the dull thuds from under the surface to know exactly where Dymas was and she used that to fuel her anger and powers.

"If you don't stand aside and go running back to your master," she addressed the squat, pale green goblin in a voice which meant serious business, "I will personally send you back to the time when goblins were hunted for their blood and flesh by all witches and warlocks and let them boil you alive."

The goblin blinked its cream-coloured eyes before gulping, "You aren't strong enough to do that." The thing's voice was unsure and held a high note of fear. "Master says so."

Shooting a hand forward, Tyra grabbed the creature by one of its elongated ears and hoisted it up, "Really, now?"

With her free hand, the spirit called forth a spectral mirror which shimmered in its unnatural existence before showing a large cooking pot that bubbled and boiled with a heavy green liquid that was being stirred by a vicious-looking crone with a hooked nose, warts and wild manic eyes that danced about as if constantly looking for something.

The creature screamed and tried to wriggle away which made Tyra smirk devilishly. "Going to be a good boy and run along?" she teased before letting out a yell as the goblin bit down hard upon her hand.

In a fluid motion, Tyra released the goblin from her grasp and kicked the creature hard so that it went flying across the garden and into a solid wall with a sickening crunch before smearing down with a long trail of green.

"Tyra!" Dyma's terrified and panicked call brought the spirit back into the moment followed briefly by some scrabbling noises. "Tyra!"

"Dymas!" the spirit called back. She scanned around, spotting a small hole in the black ice and quickly thrust her hand in, blindly searching for the volf. "I'm here, I'm going to get you out. I just need to know that you're—"

Nearly jumping in surprise when two hands viciously grabbed a tight hold upon hers, the spirit bit back a yell of pain as a series of half-formed, panic-filled words reached her ears. Dymas was clearly freaking out as the water level must have been rising quicker now.

"Hang on, just a few moments longer," she murmured against the pain, knowing full well that the grip was one of someone fearing that they were going to die.

Grabbing the edge of the small hole with the tips of the fingers of her free hand, the spirit concentrated for a few seconds before feeling the resistance of the ice. Someone clearly had the notion that she would try to help the boy and had taken advantage of every spell they could think of to ensure that he didn't get released that way. For a second she cursed, hating the fact that Cresta was wising up to her ticks, then suddenly a sharp panic shot through her system as she felt Dyma's grip on her hand lessen just a fraction.

With no real plan in mind, Tyra did the only thing that she was able to do in the given circumstances. Throwing herself into the infinite layers of reality that she could access, the spirit let herself fall through the invisible walls before pulling herself forcibly back out and into the freezing, choking water. For a second she was disorientated, but then a lifeless body crashed into her and she clung on to him desperately.

Her lips slammed onto Dymas's, forcing air back into his lungs and startling the boy enough that he hazily opened his amber eyes to find out what was going on before immediately panicking once again. Tyra grabbed the sides of his face to hold him still, blowing another breath of air into his body whilst casting her eyes up to the surface of the pond. There was no way out of that place and she very nearly wanted to huff out loud, but managed to stop herself.

Releasing another breath into the volf's body, Tyra made a choice and closed her eyes, concentrating harshly as this was a very dangerous jump she was attempting and there was no time available to really choose a location. Thankfully she remembered that there was an old summer house in the grounds of the mountains, surrounded by a small forest and it would more than likely suffice for their needs now.

There was no way to tell Dymas to brace himself but she held him close to her body and breathed for him one last time before the pond glowed brightly with blinding white light that cracked the ice and dispersed the darkness around it to reveal the hidden beauty that still lay beneath.

As the light faded, revealing that the pond was now empty of the two captives the Worshiper stepped from his hidden alcove with a bemused smile on his features, "So the spirit is the golden guardian? That is something very useful to know."

Crashing down on the rough icy ground, Tyra rolled as much as she possibly could in order to break the fall for the boy before coming to an abrupt stop due to a large rock. Forgetting the pain that was coursing through her own body, Tyra placed Dymas onto his back and leaned her ear against his chest. There was a heartbeat, faint and unsure and the spirit pulled herself upright to place her hand on his lips. Nothing.

No breath escaped from Dymas's lips and the spirit shook her head before snapping, "Oh no you don't." Quickly she raised his head back and once again placed her lips onto his, breathing heavily into his body and feeling his chest rise just underneath her elbow.

On the fourth inhalation of breath, Dymas's amber eyes shot open and water gushed up from his mouth. Quickly he turned onto his side, coughing violently as the water tried to escape from his lungs so that good wholesome air could replace it. He was vaguely aware of the arms around him, the soft voice coaxing him to relax and breathe normally, but the world was still very much a blur.

"T-Tyra?" he managed to stammer out a good minute later, twisting onto his back with a wince of pain and glad to find himself being held by the spirit. "What are we doing?"

"Escaping, my prince," Tyra said, placing a passionate kiss onto those fine lips that were thankfully regaining their usual darker colouring. "Though after we take a moment to warm you up and get rid of any residual water from your lungs, of course."

Dymas made spluttering sounds and pointed behind her, but the spirit presumed that he was just being his usual worried self and picked the boy up into her arms like a chivalrous hero in an old fairy tale before turning around with the intention of heading straight into the summer house so that she could get her prince settled safely down for the approaching daylight and run him a hot bath.

Only the way to the summer house was blocked by the now all too familiar figure of Brutus with his grey skin and pigeon-feathered hair, together with at least fifty of his best gargoyles. Tyra wanted to make a snarky comment towards them, she really did but already she was aware that there were at least ten others moving stealthily in behind her to cut off any possible retreat. If she wanted to escape with Dymas right now, she would have to fight her way out as her body had not regained the power used for the last jump and Dymas was far too heavy in her arms to be of much use in a battle right now.

"Dammit!" the spirit cursed, causing Brutus to grin a little as he signalled for his men to move in and chain the pair up.

Chapter 5

Sworn to Protect

Shivering ever so slightly, despite having been wrapped up in what could pass as a blanket, Dymas snuggled just a little closer to Tyra, hating the fact that he was being so weak. There were many things that he would willingly do to these monsters if he had half the chance, but with his limbs still half frozen and with Tyra's insistence that he did not over-exert himself right now, the volf was rather unfortunately stuck.

Gently his fingers ran over the other's body, remembering all the times that they had been together and almost longing for that powerful, dangerous touch from his spirit protector. He would give anything in the world to be far away from here right now, somewhere safe and warm where the snow was on the outside whilst he could just remain snugly in bed with his lover, not caring for the night.

A hiss escaped as his finger caught on an upraised part of the length of wire that was wound around the girl's torso in homage to a duty she had sworn herself to, so many hundreds of years ago that it was impossible to tell what it originally was. The soft blue eyes, those which he had fallen in love with after a period of hating them, turned quietly down to his strange amber ones which were currently locked on the small droplets of red blood which was flowing from the cut.

"Are you hungry, Dymas?" Tyra whispered softly, running her hand through the tangled white hair and wondering just how the gargoyles had known where her teleportation would materialize when even she couldn't always predict such a thing. Especially when using it as a means of unplanned escape. It was something that made her feel rather worried but for reasons that she could not really focus on. Tyra hated being out of the loop on something, or unaware of what was going on in the background, but in this situation there wasn't really a lot that she could do about it in the long run. Instead she focused her attention on Dymas, knowing that if the volf was hungry then he would have to be fed and that could prove to be a problem, given the company that they were currently keeping.

Dymas tried to shake his head, to pass off the dryness in his throat as an extension of the freezing water he had been subjected to and not anything else. He tried not to look into the spirit's ever-changing eyes, despite knowing already that Tyra would fully know his mood. It was an obnoxious trait sometimes that the other possessed, especially as it only appeared to focus down on him, but Tyra was his lover and looked after him so much it only made sense that she would be able to read him like a book.

"I'm starving," he finally admitted, gripping his hand into a tight fist to stop staring at the cut. "But I cannot feed yet, I must resist."

"Why?" Tyra sounded exasperated already and they hadn't even begun to argue properly yet. One of the problems with

Dymas was that despite his resolute behaviour that he would never give into the pain of the torture which had been inflicted upon his body and mind since virtually the day of his birth, sometimes the young volf would just take the punishments and tortures or else deprive himself of something that he desperately needed because he believed that it would help someone. Tyra had lost track of the amount of times they had argued over the volf not feeding correctly and she really wasn't in the mood to deal with it all now.

Opening one amber eye to look at Tyra with an expression of almost incomprehension, Dymas sighed long and hard. "Do you want me to be poisoned?"

Glancing over at the gargoyles, who were gathering together to form an odd sort of nest-like infrastructure to keep themselves warm, as well as block the entrance to the cave that they were hunkering down in for the day, the spirit had to pause for a fraction of a second to remember that for Dymas drinking certain types of blood was like drinking bleach. The gargoyles created by Cresta had a vile-smelling blue blood that had once nearly caused Dymas to be burned from the inside out and ever since the volf had never dared to drink from the vile creatures.

"You know I would never wish such a thing on you." The spirit's voice was soft, lips barely moving as she wrapped her arms softly around Dymas's form. "I was offering myself, actually."

Letting out a gurgle of surprise, which was thankfully covered by Brutus braying loudly at some antics going on between two hatchlings, Dymas stared up at Tyra in shock for a second or two before his eyes narrowed seductively. "Now that's a proposition that I couldn't refuse."

Without thinking of where they were, their present company or even the situation Tyra automatically leaned down, pulling the still rather cold volf up to meet her fine lips in a passionate kiss, chuckling lightly when the boy shifted their position so that she was straddling the volf. Their kisses became more heated, tongues dancing back and forth across one another in a familiar way which both had sorely missed as in this moment in time there were no illusions, no trickery or distractions from their little happy bubble of a real expression of their emotions.

"Tyra," Dymas breathed heavily, pulling back from the kiss after a few long seconds in an almost desperate need for air. "Ta—"

Tyra gently placed a finger on the boy's lips, lightly shushing him as she shook her head, trying not to giggle too loudly, "I didn't know that you were into voyeurism."

Dymas moaned a little, hardly able to miss the other's free hand running teasingly down the inside of his leg, "I'm not, but I need you right now." The spirit would have laughed at that statement because his eagerness for her flesh was very apparent at the moment but her blue eyes had noticed someone approaching them.

"You're in a state close to blood frenzy, you need to drink my prince," Tyra said, her tone cool and neutral as she slowly slid down the sides of her top to expose her neck and chest to the other before pulling him closer to her body. "Drink Dymas, drink deep and long."

It took no second bidding for Dymas to extend his fangs and pierce the flesh just above the female's collarbone. Softly and with care his hands wound their way around to her broad back in order to rest perfectly against the rough skin that was far more appealing to the volf than the soft silk that he had felt last time they had done this. It was strange to think that he could compare the two instances, but it wasn't that hard to do. Especially when drinking the strange spirit blood that ranged in colour from grey to black and was unique in taste.

Very few vampires could stand to drink it, saying that it was either too addictive or tasted like ash. Dymas thought that Tyra's blood tasted like an old vintage wine which had been dug up from the cellar and had to be savoured because it was rare and only drank in very small amounts. A shiver passed through his body as the life-giving liquid coursed through his throat and unbidden his hips ground up towards the female's.

Brutus came to a commanding stop, glaring down at the spirit who was glaring back at him with ease and clearly content to allow Dymas to rut against her lower body without even the smallest hint of shame showing on her face. He sneered and threw an additional blanket at them with a scoff of disgust. "Keep it down, I don't want to be disturbed by your vile noises all day."

"Ironic, coming from a creature who knows nothing of what happens during the day," the spirit shot back, smirking slightly as the gargoyle stalked off back to his guards to be instantly forgotten as the toxins from the bite managed to bring her pleasure, which caused a little moan of satisfaction to escape from her lips. Tilting her head back a little further, the spirit silently closed her eyes to allow the boy to drink. Dymas took deep, long mouthfuls of the warm blood, relieved that the other had firmly grounded herself in this level of reality. The black substance flowed down his throat, swishing around in an intoxicating mess of liquids and fuelling his aching bones, muscles and stirring just slightly the powers hidden within him.

If the hunger had been any worse, Dymas could have easily drained Tyra of every last drop of blood within her body. Though he never wanted to drain the spirit to the point where she would no longer be able to come back to this realm, for it would just break his heart into a million different pieces, which, unfortunately, his godforsaken mother knew all too well.

Full of the enticing blood and feeling more than a little daring, Dymas slowly retracted his fangs from the supple flesh before sealing the wound with a gentle lick. "Take me there," he whispered, low and conspiratorially. "Take me now."

Almost without bidding, despite normally being highly reserved about this particular issue, Tyra increased her grip on the male volf and gently rested her forehead against his, blue eyes focused straight onto amber.

There was a momentary pain and then a sense of falling straight down through the rocks below them into a quiet abyss of welcoming nothingness. After a few long seconds Dymas reopened his eyes to find himself in a long, richly furnished room with a roaring fire at one end and a dark mahogany four-poster bed covered by red silk blankets and gold-lined cushions.

Paintings hung on the walls, but only of the people that he wished to always look upon. His elder brother Mephistopheles looking young and grand with his beautiful wife on his arm and several smaller images of his niece and nephew thought they were rather obscured, because he was never overly sure if he had truly seen them or not.

The other picture was of his sister, though as he turned his gaze upon it a frown rippled across his features. Normally, Ekata would be as he remembered her, a little five-year-old child who would be hiding behind something with only her glorious amber eyes showing, because he knew that they would never change. However, Ekata now looked to be more like a young lady of olden times, dressed in an elegant yet beautifully simple white dress with long flowing sleeves. Her long ebony-black hair was brushed back and held in place with flowers and she smiled so radiantly that Dymas could have sworn she was in love. A male figure, dressed in worn, battered-looking leather and carrying a large broadsword stood next to her looking tall and proud; as well as more than ready to slew anyone who meant to do her harm.

"Tyra," Dymas whispered, knowing that the spirit was behind him without having to turn around, "Who is that man with my sister?"

Instead of receiving a response, all the volf got was the feeling of Tyra stepping up right behind him and gently bringing her hands around his body before lacing her fingers with his own. Gently they began caressing his stomach and slowly creeping up his chest. Dymas had to sigh because he could easily feel what state of dress she was in and it was infuriatingly distracting. "You are annoying when you do this."

"Of course, my prince," Tyra whispered, gently twisting the boy around and smiling at him, "but that is the way that I shall always be with you."

Settling himself into the hold more naturally, Dymas was about to comment when he caught sight of his arm. Instead of his usual rags or that horrible black top he had been forced to wear, there was a very fine golden sleeve that was made out of a material that softly shimmered. Gently he pushed himself back, not so far that he was out of the spirit's reach but enough that he could glance down with relatively little hassle. He was more than surprised to find himself in an outfit which was fit for a prince in olden times. It was far more trimmed and less floozy than the pictures and paintings he had seen, but was finely decorated with golden thread and blood-red rubies. Unfortunately, there was no cloak as he expected there to be but as he cast his eyes once again around the room he spotted it hanging neatly up in the corner on a rather ornate stand.

Something snagged at his neck as he turned back to ask the spirit just what was going on and carefully he withdrew a silver necklace which made the breath in his lungs catch in his throat. It was a heavy chain bearing a single pendant of the cross of the Knights Templar, encircled with a ring of gold set with a black gemstone. Confusion settled quickly in Dymas's mind and he looked up at his lover. "Tyra, what is this?"

"I'm not sure," the spirit responded gently, looking around the room as if she had just realized that it was not all of her own creation. She barely appeared to notice that she was now dressed as if she were a warrior Priestess of the Realm, though Dymas very much doubted that many of her order wore their uniforms in quite the way she currently had hers set. Her blue eyes turned back to the amber ones. “It feels like we have been here before but I cannot say where we are.”

Dymas slowly swallowed before shuddering. “Tell me this is real, not just some figment of our imagination.”

Stepping forward quickly, Tyra lifted the boy’s chin with her fingers and placed a kiss on those fine lips. The touch was softer than she remembered in a long while and ancient memories stirred within the spirit’s head. A sigh of relief, long and feeling as though it had been held in since beyond the days of her self-awareness came to be, escaped her and her fingers ran lovingly through the longer white locks which she had wanted to hold for so very long, “Finally I re-find you, my most missed prince.”

“And I you, even though we were so blind as to not see what was standing right in front of us,” Dymas whispered back, feeling a shudder go through his body, though not understanding why. Maybe it had something to do with Tyra gently scratching his black wolf ears? “Why did you not reveal yourself before? You must have known for such a very long time.”

Tyra smiled, knowingly but with a stronger purpose involved than the volf would ever be able to guess and sighed once again, “Because I have been tricked once before in my search for you. I had to be sure this time… I am sworn to protect you throughout all of time itself, until the final days, but it is not always easy to find you in this world.”

“How do you know I am me?” Dymas asked, still looking intently at the now Priestess that stood before him and feeling the need to be with her, despite already knowing that they had been together more than once before.

Lightly their lips re-touched, slowly getting stronger and more passionate whilst he waited on his answer with patience and dedication. "Say my true name, my lord, and then you will have your answer," the spirit whispered gently, keeping their bodies close but not quite touching.

The volf frowned for a second, not quite understanding the question before a smile crossed his features. "Tynan Thane, of the Western Arch of the Sky and Sun."

A sudden shudder went through Tyra, a lively jolt that seemed to make all of her muscles contract and expand in the same second. For a moment or two, the spirit was silent, focusing on her breathing. She blinked several times and then stared in surprise at Dymas before pulling him into a tight, passionate embrace. Then she threw her legs around his waist and allowed him to carry her to the bed. They lay together for a long time, passionate sounds filling the room though only they were there to hear them.

Chapter 6

Darkness or Light

Becoming aware of the bitter cold around him, Dymas slowly prised open his amber eyes and stared out at the snow strewn field. A frown crossed his features, the scent of fresh blood invading his nose and making him want to retch violently. Slowly he pushed himself up, trying to make sense of it all. There were so many bodies, wolves for the most part with their heads sliced clean off and guts spilled out onto the ground. He tried desperately not to throw up what little he had eaten, but it was hard staring down at so many dead bodies. "Dymas," a voice whispered on the wind, "run." Turning sharply, Dymas snarled and moved into a natural fighting stance, "I do not fear you anymore, Mother! Stop with the games, I'm already sick of them."

"Run, Dymas, run," the voice, devoid of any trait to make it recognizable to him continued on. "Run now, whilst you still have the chance."

Turning with a snarl, the male felt his body shift a little as the beast within wanted nothing more than to be free. He forced it back under control, however, upon seeing a figure clothed in a brilliant black gown that looked like it had been woven out of the fabric of night itself. The figure's head hung low and long strands of messy black hair curled towards the blood-soaked snow beneath the bare feet. Two white wolf ears shifted slightly back and forth as if listening for the approach of someone.

"Ekata?" he questioned softly. "What have you done?"

Slowly the matching amber eyes rose to meet his own and he saw nothing but complete and total despair in their depths. He took a step back, frowning slightly. "What happened? Ekata answer me…"

"How could you?" the voice came again, so soft, so timid, the voice of a terrified child. "How could you do this…"

"Ekata?" Dymas questioned again before feeling a very strong metallic taste in his mouth. Looking down at his hands, the volf paled. They were covered in blood and he quickly turned back to his sister. "No… I didn't do this! I would never want this!"

"Liar." The voice coming out of Ekata was now devoid of emotion, her amber eyes swirling with red and silver whilst her hand rose up. "You wanted nothing but to destroy everything. You were born to destroy everything!"

Within seconds the female twin was at her brother's throat, the despair-filled eyes not even flinching as he felt the long clawed nails dig into his chest. "Shall I rip out your heart and feed it to the dogs like you threatened to do? Or shall I make you watch as it slowly stops beating in the palm of my hand?"

A hand snapped forward, suddenly latching onto the girl's neck and for a second Dymas didn't comprehend that it was him. A snarl of laughter escaped his throat. "As if I would willingly allow her to give into the inner darkness of her heart, release your hold on her."

Ekata chuckled, the eyes bulging slightly with the pressure that was being applied. "You will make her take the darkness in you, that is fated." The voice wasn't his sister's, that much he knew, but he didn't trust a word that it was saying either. "She will become far greater in using it than you ever will."

"But from darkness comes a light." The volf smirked towards the now shuddering figure. "One that cannot be replaced."

"Don't think that you know anything, you are the destroyer of the light and nothing you can do will ever change that, volf." The creature slithered a little, loosening its hold on its current form. "You seek to do more than just spill innocent blood and you will do so in order to devour the world and make it yours. And when you are done, you will make her take the darkness and destroy everything. Just like you're going to do with me."

Slowly Dymas straightened himself out and let go of the creature that crashed onto the snow-covered ground. Glancing down at the pathetic mass, Dymas shook his head, "I only kill what I need to survive and I repent for those lives I take. Darkness is only Light shaded and Light is only a brighter shade of Darkness. You are nothing but a repellent pest who feeds off negative emotions to drive those who had not faced their inner darkness to despair."

The creature snarled, "You won't leave here without killing me, boy!"

"On the contrary." The Volf's amber eyes flicked up to another figure who just lingered on the edge of the blood stained snow. "I was never here."

Turning, the creature let out a yelp as a warhammer was slammed into the ground just in front of it, a loud crackle of thunder bouncing around the hills above them.

"Boo," Tyra said grimly to the creature, watching as it paled and disappeared into its own level of the astral plains. "Little guttersnipes, biggest pain in the neck once they get going. Good thing you've encountered them before, my prince."

"How did you get in here, Tyra? I thought that you couldn't generally cut into someone else's plane of reality easily?"

The priestess tilted her head, "There's always something unexpected."

Dymas glanced briefly, seeing a couple standing not too far off in the snow-strewn field though appearing to be frozen in time. Neither were looking at the pair, instead they seemed to be staring off into the distance, embraced in each other's arms, cloaks swirling in the breeze which for them had temporarily frozen. They were the exact same couple from the painting in Tyra's personal realm and Dymas almost felt tears prickling at his eyes.

The spirit took tight hold of the young Volf's hand, "You crave to see her that much?"

"No, I crave for her to be happy and free," Dymas closed his eyes slowly, "Away from this madness even though I know she will be drawn ever closer."

"We've moved," Tyra said, sighing a little as she looked upwards to probably glance at the real world. "Don't be too surprised if we aren't somehow back in the Manor when we wake up."

Unusually, an odd sort of smirk crossed the Volf's face. "With Mother leering over us, no doubt."

A painfully bright light cut through the artificial snow plain to bring the real one back into horrible biting focus. Peeling his eyes open, Dymas felt initially confused as the view was rather pleasant to behold. He was deep inside a garden filled with the most stunning white lilies that he had ever seen that stretched out all around him. Was he really waking up or was this some other vile dream that was being thrust upon him by the spirit realm that longed to claim his soul? Next time he fancied being with Tyra for any length of time, he would do so in reality and keep the guttersnipes out of his way. However, his confirmation of the real world came from an all too unpleasant sight that sparked fear in his heart.

Cresta Du Winter approached from across the greenery, wearing a black gown with a matching veil. In her hands she held a bouquet of dead lilies tied with a blood-red ribbon and was flanked by two of the gargoyles, who were carrying a body of a young woman with long black hair and impossibly pale skin. The girl was weak-looking and was clearly unconscious, dressed in a simple white dress that complimented her perfectly.

Dymas, still not fully awake, stared in shock towards Cresta before desperately trying to scramble towards the held figure. "No, please, no!"

"Oh? To what exactly?" Cresta responded, signalling for her guards to drop the now comatose body onto the ground. She ignored Akira, who was tasked with carrying the spirit entrapment jar which must have been holding Tyra, judging by the way that it was shining brightly with a thousand different colours – the enraged spirit was clearly attempting to break free. "Your dinner which I am thoughtfully providing for you since that human priest has proved himself to be completely useless. Whether you like it or not, the day draws ever closer to when I will draw out that power within you—"

"Even if you weren't my mother I would call you insane," Dymas virtually spat, attempting to scurry towards the fallen girl to make sure that it wasn't his sister, "There is no power within me!"

A sharp slap was delivered to his face and for the first time the male volf realized that he was chained with ancient manacles to a pair of oak trees which would not yield easily. He hissed towards the fair-looking woman, feeling his fangs retract to be replaced by the sharp jaws of a canine and the inner beast struggle desperately to break from the self-imposed cage. For a second it was so tempting, just to be that free and that strong but Dymas knew that he couldn't let such a thing happen. If he did, then he would only end up in Cresta's control.

The vampiric woman smiled one of her rare, childlike smiles and she knelt down in front of her bastard son with an expression of calm, controlled and unconditional love, "Oh my sweet Dymas, you try to hide yourself behind a wall of emotions but you were always the one who was easiest to read. You claim indifference and shut down, but you wear your heart on your sleeve and it makes everything so much easier to torment you with." Her voice was filled with so much evil that Dymas wanted nothing more than to rip her to pieces. "You say you have no power within you, yet your body betrays you… even more so now that she has started her approach back towards you.”

Taking a snapping bite towards Cresta, a snarl forming but dying in his throat, the boy saw the proof that the crazy vampire was talking about in front of his eyes. The golden swirls had begun to glow and shimmer far greater than before. They were more defined that his sisters, he knew that much, outlined with a steady black line as if someone had cruelly painted them onto his body against his will. Whether he was prepared to accept it or not, the fabled prince was making his presence known as the maiden returned to his side. “You don’t have her,” he snapped, trying to be defiant and his usual arrogant self as the girl who had been delivered to him was human, he recognized the scent now.

He was still determined to knock Cresta off her proud perch though. “If you did then you would be in a world of trouble because she has her—”

Shivering in shock as the ice-cold hands of his mother suddenly found the sides of his face, Dymas was quite unprepared to find himself almost transported to a wood that he didn’t know. It was dark and dank, surrounded by a large bog which stank to high hell even in this brief vision. Fire suddenly erupted, white and glistening, and there came the howls and desperate pleas although he couldn’t focus on where they were coming from. He paled when a tall figure emerged from the centre of the flames, carrying someone who was thin and dressed in borrowed clothes. Black hair stood out against the pure white flames and whilst the eyes were closed, he knew that they were amber. Terror filled him as he glanced up at the figure, praying to see some young wolf with sharp piercing silver eyes but instead met with the pale grey, ghost eyes of a man destroyed so long ago.

There was a howl filled with pain and brimming with anger and from the depths of the flames a wolf, almost as black as the night around it, burst forth and charged towards the figure. Teeth bared, silver eyes blazing with a furry and for a second Dymas believed that he would make it. Then a swirl of red and blue slammed straight into the creature's side, sending him sprawling back into the flames and quite possibly into a nearby tree with a splintering crunch that weakened his resolve beyond anything that he had previously seen.

"No!" he screamed aloud, uncharacteristically feeling so helpless and useless despite being aware that this was probably happening hundreds of miles away from him, "Let her go! Please, don't try and do what you are doing to me! You'll kill her!"

The freezing hands were suddenly gone from his face and the darkness faded, being replaced by the fake green lush that was whatever hell this was. A groan escaped him, one that he had not felt for the longest time and slowly his eyes travelled up towards Cresta who stared back at him blankly, "You do not know what games you are playing woman. You will see us all dead before you achieve what you foolishly desire."

"And when you are dead," Cresta replied with her soft calmness as she rose to a standing position, "I shall take all of that power from your lifeless bodies and simply use it for my own purpose."

Snapping her fingers, the guards and Akira disappeared like shadows and the greenery faded away to an ashen black of destruction, “Do you recognize this place now? What you did here that time?”

Dymas tried not to look but couldn’t help himself. He remembered this place now; it had been an inner sanctum for the Du Winter children, a place where his once loving elder brother would sometimes bring them to play when his mother had not been as crazed as she was now. How one day something had happened whilst they were at play, all he had been able to describe it as at the time was that someone had tried to steal his twin away from him.

The flames of his anger and fear had engulfed the entire room, caused his vampire sister to go insane and severely burn his loving elder brother. Cresta grinned. “Linger here with your guilt and savour the moment when your precious sister will give her life up to save you. You are destruction, Dymas, it is what you were born to do and what you will always do, regardless of what you believe.”

The woman turned and disappeared from view, leaving the volf alone in the ashes of his guilt. Gently he shook his head, dispelling the annoying tears that threatened to overspill from his already stinging eyes. “No, no, I didn’t mean to cause this. I never… she would never… I would never… no. We are not like they say… we are not.”

Looking up at the ceiling of the inner dome, Dymas gave in and let the tears fall down the side of his face in long rivers, “Mephi, if you are there, if you can hear me, please, please don’t let that happen. Stop it, give her back to the wolf… don’t bring her here. I won’t let her take the darkness for me.”

That could be the only thing that saves the pair of you, though. A voice, one that was familiar but not recognized, spoke inside his head and caused the volf to baulk in surprise. *Sometimes the darkest route is the only way to escape the darkness that you are facing.*

"She is light, though," he whispered aloud, hanging his head in shame and not worrying about the fact that he would appear to be talking to himself. "She is creation…"

Silver kills werewolves, yet she is more wolf than you. Gold has no effect on either race.

Dymas snarled, trying to push the voice away though not really sure where it came from. "If she is not light, then what is she?"

What does light do to virtually all supernatural creatures?

"Destroys us all." Dymas repeated the old mantra which some teacher had drilled into him briefly when Cresta had been prepared to give the twins lessons. Dymas was about to argue when he felt his heart constrict.

"Light destroys us all…"

Chapter 7

The Night of Fire

The smallest tinkling of glass gave Tyra some form of renewed hope as she continued her tirade against the wall which was slowly draining her powers with every attempt, but the spirit was not about to give up that easily. She had gone through far too much to be defeated by such a small and insignificant thing as a piece of motley glass. Though even she knew that despite her stubbornness the glass would not yield to anyone easily. Eldered glass had been designed to contain the most powerful of astral presences and ensure that they were pretty much rendered as harmless as could be. In some ways she wished that she had never had the misfortune to come across the stuff, else this whole endeavour wouldn't feel like such a waste of time, but knew that she had to keep persisting. If after so many hours of constant struggle she had managed to create a tiny fracture in one layer, surely she could get through the rest of them and break out of this jar.

But exhaustion was already beginning to prey on her mind, whilst she was ethereal and had more than the average human's strength and stamina to keep on going through the relentless task, there were limits to what she could achieve.

Added to the fact that the eldered glass drained her life force as well despite remaining completely clear at all times, Tyra knew that she was in a terrible spot. Raising her hand high above her head, she smashed down with all her might on the tiny crack and felt rather than saw the yellow-coloured shock wave that slammed her into the opposite side of the jar, causing it to shift slightly. She cursed, snarling as the small crack repaired itself. "Damn whoever to the seventh level of hell for creating this prison!"

The spirit flopped to her knees, wanting nothing more than to just screech obscenities to all the possible gods above for what they were putting her through, but knew it was pointless. To an outsider, Tyra would look like nothing more than a small fairy or at least a very rude approximation of one, who was trapped inside of a jar to be gawked at throughout the centuries. She was trapped; she knew it and it drove her to the virtual limits of her patience to think that there was next to nothing that she could do about it. "Some guardian I am," she mused to herself, at long last spitting some blood from the back of her throat as she reground herself in the reality behind the glass, "I can't even…"

Casting her oddly coloured eyes out of the jar, Tyra sighed heavily at the sight of Dymas chained up like some prisoner with his hands high above his head and no one to comfort him in the persisting rain that dribbled in through the broken roof. The spirit didn't want to try to think what the volf was thinking about at that point in time, as she was sure that it was some horrid memory brought on by this nightmare-ridden place. The glass felt like ice under her fingers as she desperately tried to reach out to the other. "I'm here, Dymas, even though I know you can't hear me right now. I'm here for you."

For a second she believed that the male volf had heard her, his black ears twitching at the sound of her voice and the spirit felt a smile almost creep to her lips. But then Dymas started screaming, a genuinely terrified scream the likes of which he had not let past his lips since the day of the fire.

Amber eyes snapped open in panic, bringing the dark and burnt-out room into focus once again and taking away the heat which had been stripping the flesh from his bones. He had to remain focused, had to try and remain in the present and not dwell on the past, but how could he be expected to do something like that when the entire world around him was nothing more than a haunting memory?

Even the presence of the chains around his wrists did little to alleviate the memories that were plaguing his mind and a bitter sting of tears began to form in the corner of his eyes. "No," he ground out, "No, I will not remember. I will not…"

The memories surfaced all too quickly despite his attempts to hide from them, the shadows of the scorched black world filtering back to lighter woods and exquisite-looking paintings that must have taken some master craftsman years to finish. Though most of them were obscured from view by hundreds of different toys that covered virtually every available surface. There were dolls, bears, wooden soldiers, building blocks, balls and any other number of items to keep even the most hyperactive child amused for hours upon end.

"Dy-dy?" a voice, young and sweet caught Dymas's attention and, tearfully, he turned his head to find a young girl with short, very messy black hair, large amber eyes and two very small white wolf ears protruding from the top of her head. She was dressed in what looked like a very well handed down brown dress with several different patches roughly sewn onto it and she had the biggest grin on her face. "Found you, Dy-dy!"

The tiny five-year-old Ekata giggled and ran towards her brother, wrapping her arms around his neck and hugging him. For a second Dymas was confused as he was sure there was no way that a five-year-old girl should have been able to hug him, but then remembered the fact that he was also five years old and that they were exactly the same height. "No fair, Eky!" he half yelped back against the hug. "You cheated!"

"Did not!" Ekata responded to her brother, before grinning and lightly touching his arm. "Tag! You're it!" She took off, running through the large room and making a grab for a couple of colourful sheets that they had been using to build a fort before they had opted to change the game to one of hide and seek, a game which had now turned into tag. Sometimes children's imaginations were far too much to keep up with, but the vampire watching over the pair couldn't be happier.

Neither could the white-haired volf, because here the ground was covered with a soft carpet and there was a large bouncy bed covered with silken sheets of pink and red that had proper curtains to pull around and make everything nice and cozily dark. It was a far cry from their usual dwellings of a small dark room with a rickety old iron bed and a window which leaked during the rain and always let in just a slither of sunlight, which had to be avoided at all costs by Dymas who was more sensitive to sunlight that his sister.

There were books too, a whole library full to his infant eyes even though it was merely a few shelves that had been slung up some time ago, and it was a place that felt so wonderful that he never wanted to leave it. Dymas loved the fact that their big brother would bring them here as often as he could, Mephistopheles was always saying that they deserved the chance to play, but the young volf always suspected that just maybe there was another reason for the elder vampire's visits to the room.

But at that moment in time, Dymas was more concerned with chasing his twin and trying to catch her in their swapped-over game of tag. Being so young the games could change from one second to the next and it was fun just being able to run around being silly. If their mother had been present, then they would have had to have been on their best behaviour because she didn't like naughty children and especially seemed to have it in for them. Maybe they had been really naughty when they were first born, or they had done something to make her not like them? Dymas did not know why, but he was able to know at that young age that his mother was not to be messed with or disobeyed and he'd do anything to keep Ekata safe.

Dashing around the corner of one of the boxes, Dymas took a leaping dive towards his sister but slightly misjudged and, as the girl squealed happily away, the young volf ended up crashing straight into Siren, who yelped as they went tumbling to the floor in a great big heap.

"Ow!" Siren yelled, pushing the boy away from her. "Watch where you are going, idiot!"

Her long curls of flaming red hair made the young vampire look huge in comparison and Dymas curled up in fright as Siren continued to yell at him. “You could’ve killed me!”

“Siren.” Mephistopheles’s voice came across, firm but fair. “Don’t go yelling like that. They’re only playing. You used to do the same to me when you were that age.”

The girl glared in response, “I did not. I wouldn’t go running around like a half-blind monkey and knock people over.”

Sighing, Mephistopheles stared at his red-haired sister and wondered what this whole situation was really all about. He had a fair idea but he wasn’t going to press the matter overly much as the girl was on the verge of telling him what was wrong with her, throwing a massive tantrum or else bursting into tears. He had hoped that spending some time with the twins would help her to come to terms with what was bothering her, but apparently life was never going to be that easy.

“Siren, don’t start name calling, it’s not a pleasant thing for a young lady to be doing.” Maybe a little bit of tutoring would help the young vampire to calm down, as apparently she had been doing very well in her studies as of late, but Mephistopheles clearly had forgotten one small fact about his little sister.

“Don’t you dare call me that!” Siren half-screamed at her older brother, barely able to contain the rage inside her small frame. “I don’t want to be a young lady! I don’t want to have to live by all of those rules! You can’t make me do it… you’re just as bad as—”

"Si!" Tugging on Siren's sleeve, Ekata looked up at her big sister with wide eyes.

Siren turned and snapped harshly towards the youngster, "What?"

Ekata blinked, looking a little more than terrified, but then grinned and offered her a rather mangled looking teddy bear which had clearly seen better days. "Mister Bear wants to play!"

"Well, I don't," Siren snapped again. "Bears are for little kids."

"You're not much bigger than me," the five-year-old replied earnestly.

Mephistopheles tried to stifle the laugh that wanted to escape him, but pretty much failed as the sibling argument continued on between the two girls.

"That's not what I meant, you little runt!"

"But you said—"

"Gah! When will you grow up?"

"When I'm six?"

"No! That's… oh, go away, stupid dog-rat."

"No, Mister Bear wants to play with big sis!"

"Well, I don't! Go away."

"But Mister Bear!"

"Leave me alone, Ekata! I don't want to play with you or Mister Bear!"

"Why?"

"Oh shut up!"

"But why?"

Siren let out a yell in frustration, gave Ekata a little push before scowling and storming off to try and sulk on the opposite side of the room. The little female volf blinked from her odd position on the floor, picked herself up, dusted off the teddy bear and without even a glance back at her two brothers, toddled off towards her sister to try and get the irate girl to play with her.

"Girls are scary," Dymas commented, from somewhere down besides Mephistopheles' left knee, and the elder vampire brother looked down at his strange half-mixed brother with a gentle smile. "They make too much noise."

Chuckling, Mephistopheles shook his head, "Boys are worse, trust me on that Dymas. Just you wait until you have a new baby brother running around, they'll be nothing but noise all over the place that will make them two look like they're best of friends."

Turning his amber eyes up towards Mephistopheles, Dymas blinked, "How do you know that?"

"What, that boys are noisy or that you're going to have a baby brother soon?" The vampire smiled and scooped the youngster up into his arms. "It's my little secret. I'll let you in on it when you're older…"

Before another question could be asked, however, there came the ever so gentle chiming of a clock, signalling that it was coming up to four o'clock. Mephistopheles paled slightly, his dark grey eyes widening in shock. "Siren, did you play with the clock at all?"

"No," the girl replied automatically, dropping the childish argument she had been having with her half-sister and virtually grabbing the child. "I've never touched it! Not once."

Taking a deep breath, Mephistopheles made a quick signal with his hands towards his red-haired sister. "Playtime's over, we need to get a move on."

"Maybe we'll get lucky," Siren said, scooping up the teddy bear and handing Ekata to her elder brother, ignoring the girl's complaints as she hurriedly attempted to tidy up the room to make it look like it hadn't been used by two very hyper children. "She has run late before, right?"

"Never this late," Mephistopheles said turning abruptly, the midnight black-haired vampire tried to think of the safest route through the house to get the twins back to where they were supposed to be without implicating himself or his sister in doing anything out of the ordinary. They didn't have time to tidy the room up, not in the slightest, but it was something that could be easily explained away.

The twins looked up at him with innocence in their eyes, "But Mephi, wanna play!" chimed Dymas whilst Ekata reached to snag one of the white bows on the top of Siren's head.

"Playtime's over," Mephistopheles whispered, trying to zone into the rest of the house to find out if his mother was back as of yet, "I'm sorry you two, I'm going to have to take you back to…"

"Mephistopheles," Siren was rapidly waving her hand towards him, from the main door to the playroom, "We've got to move now or else—"

"Or else what, dear sister?" the voice that came in from the door was similar to Mephistopheles but had more of a dark tone to it, the semblance of an adult being trapped inside a youth's body. "You two will be caught with those despicable creatures once again?"

Angell Du Winter glared at all of his siblings and knew that this time they had nowhere to run. In all respects he looked almost to be the double of Mephistopheles, just with lighter grey eyes and a strange blue tinge to his hair. It was almost possible to believe that they were twins, but Angell was actually younger by nearly fifty years. However he had managed to supplant the elder's position in the family and Mephistopheles knew that in this situation there was next to nothing that he could do or say that would sway Angell into keeping his mouth shut.

The other was as demented as his mother, far crueller and more devious, and was considered to be the family favourite by far. But Mephistopheles knew that he had to try, had to risk his luck just a little because otherwise he would fail in his duties. "Angell," he started only to wince when a vicious slap cut across his face despite the other having barely moved an inch, "Just let us go! You have to see the madness of this…"

"Of what, dear *little* brother?" The emphasis on 'little' really irked Mephistopheles, but he knew that it was a deliberate ploy by the other to wind him up. "The fact that a vampire holds in his arms two abominations and claims them to be family?"

"They are family." Keeping his tone level, the elder vampire felt his eyes narrowing slightly, wishing he could just smack the boy in the face to put him firmly back in his place. "And if they are such monstrous creatures, then Mother should have—"

The blow that was delivered to his body sent him crashing into the opposite wall that cracked with the pressure and forced him to drop the twins. Tendrils of smouldering hot smoke latched onto his arms and legs, burning through to his flesh in a matter of seconds and it was only pure determination that stopped him from yelling out in pain. He would not bow to his younger brother so easily; he was older and should have been able to easily bring the other under his control. But there was something different about Angell, something that was unpredictable and virtually uncontrollable at the same time.

"I won't have you bad mouthing Mother," Angell said in a pleasant tone, almost casually flicking his wrist towards Siren, who was trying to use the situation to her advantage and get the twins away. The girl didn't even get a chance to scream as she was plunged into the side of the bed, smashing her head on one of the ornately carved bedposts and tumbled down instantly to the floor.

The stench of blood automatically crept into the air and Mephistopheles stared in panic towards Siren, who was barely moving. "But I do wonder what she will do to the pair of you this time. I do hope that it is something unpleasant that will make you realize that you are wasting—"

Angell let out a sudden yell, turning to find Ekata had latched onto his leg and bitten down hard with her canine teeth. The smoke ropes were gone and Mephistopheles wasted no time in righting himself, landing a punch firmly on Angell's nose, which satisfyingly crunched before spurting blood and made a grab for his two sisters.

"Dymas!" Mephistopheles yelled, unable to see the boy for a few seconds before spotting him just behind one of the boxes. "Run!"

The boy nodded and followed the order, barely pausing to even question what was going on. Dymas had learned over the years that the best course of action to take in these situations was to follow his elder sibling's orders. Another burning sensation rocked Mephistopheles's body as the ropes returned, this time pure streams of fire that scorched his skin instantly and nothing could stop the scream that left Mephistopheles's lips.

"You can't escape from me!" Angell growled out. "I won't let you."

Glaring at his younger brother, Mephistopheles dropped the limp form of Siren for a second and flung his hand towards him. A torrent of ice was sent towards his brother and it hissed against the flames which had only just marginally increased.

"That should be my line!" Mephistopheles growled out. "You are overstepping your boundaries, brat!"

Just at that second though there was a sudden change in the air, the twisted grin from Angell that appeared for a fleeting moment caused the elder vampire to turn around. Another man, who had clearly used the fight between the brothers to his advantage, dressed in a long flowing black cloak, was in the process of taking Ekata away from the room. He could just see his mother in the doorway, looking murderously smug over the whole situation and the small girl appeared almost doll-like with glassy eyes.

"No, Twinny!" Dymas's voice ripped through the stillness which had crept over the whole room and suddenly

Mephistopheles realized that he couldn't move. He was on his knees, one arm outstretched to his brother and the other clasping at the empty air where his little sister had been not moments before.

"Give my Twinny back to me!" Dymas was screaming hysterically, trying to get at the man who was moving away from the scene without so much as a care in the world, "Come back! Twinny, come back!"

Angell chuckled, rising himself up and lightly dusting himself off. "I've barely begun to assert my power over you, brother, I shall look forward to…" His words were drowned out by an even louder scream from the little five-year-old volf.

Dymas knew that he was screaming uselessly but he had to somehow get through to his sister. She couldn't be that still, it wasn't like her to be that still and only a really bad man would make her be like that.

"Give me back my Twinny!" Dymas screamed again, this time latching onto the man in the black cloak and suddenly feeling a ripple of power going through his small body. There was a crack, almost as if the room had suddenly split in half and flames leapt up as if from the depths of hell. The room was engulfed in a matter of seconds and all the young boy could see was flames, all he could taste was smoke.

Water, ice cold and fresh from the outside world slammed onto his already sweat-slicked hair and brought him out of the terrible memories which had been plaguing him. Carefully, he raised his eyes, finding himself staring at a figure whom he wasn't sure that he could identify. "What are you doing here?" he asked aloud before his body collapsed as exhaustion filled his entire mind and plunged him into the darkest of sleeps.

Chapter 8

The Snow-Strewn Road

Shifting ever so slightly as the mud gave way under his feet, the vampire made sure to keep himself low to the ground so that a casual glance to the side would not alert anyone to his presence. Though the closer they got to that wretched manor, the more ill at ease Raphael felt. It had been an awful long time since he had been anywhere near this place and he could virtually feel his skin crawling with disgust over the whole notion.

Or maybe it was the fact that he was beginning to linger just a little too near to the spells and enchantments that would alert those within the castle that he was around? Maybe he was being just a bit too paranoid on that thought, but, since he was fairly sure that the several attempts that had been made on his and his beloved wife's life had come from none other than this place, he guessed that someone would be interested in finding out if he was near. Still his dark grey eyes scanned the carriages and the canopies, looking for any break in the chain that may just provide what they needed.

There wasn't even enough room for the last shards of moonlight to slither through undetected. Looked like the man who called himself Mephistopheles had thought of everything well in advance. "Sly fox," Raphael muttered under his breath. "I look forward to the day when I can shatter all of your illusions."

Ducking back into the shadows, the vampire swiftly disappeared from the probing view of an eagle-eyed but extremely unimaginative ghoul guard and slipped silently from shadow to shadow until he was a good several hundred metres away. He remained crouched though, following the rocks and trying to avoid any of the deep snowdrifts that could potentially hide ice below them. However, it didn't take him long to catch up with his travelling companions – not that they had actually moved a single step whilst he had scouted out the way ahead, of course.

Gently, he wriggled his nose as the damp smell of wet dog hit him and he gazed down upon the man who was supposed to be the guardian. "He's still asleep?" The question was obvious even to his ears, but Raphael had learnt not to always trust his eyes when it came to certain things.

"She still slumbers for the time being." Another man spoke with a voice which held age and power to it, but came out slightly cracked and filled with a tinge of worry, "They are more connected than even I had guessed. It shouldn't be long until he awakens, but I don't particularly feel like explaining to him the full extent of the situation, Raphael."

A cheeky smirk crossed the midnight black-haired man's face. "You had no troubles divulging it all to me, old man."

"Cheeky young scamp." The smile that was delivered was genuine and reminiscent of a past that Raphael didn't quite know if he remembered correctly or not, "But you are right.

There again you're only tangentially involved with the Silver Maiden, so I suppose it was easier for me to tell you about the situation."

Raphael glanced down at the slumbering werewolf, noting the look of distress on the boy's face and wondering if he had once shared the same expression. "Is this really a wise move, Alcarde? I mean I know he has to do this but…" he paused, trying to think of how best to word what he was thinking, "It feels wrong."

Alcarde didn't reply for a few long moments. Instead the washed-out eyes stared across the land in front of them to the vampires that they were tracking and, in the distance, the Manor of the Du Winters. His age seemed more prominent, the wrinkled lines of his face deeper and the shadows darker. His white hair stood out against the snow, almost purer that the frozen particles of water but his dark blue eyes bore into the soul and left an impression that was hard to ignore. They were the eyes of a father, long forgotten and still terribly missed.

Seeming to come to himself, Alcarde gently handed the slumbering Fiero to Raphael and shook his head, "This whole situation is wrong. But fate has dealt us these cards and we must act upon them as best as we can, Raphael. You are right though; I am playing a dangerous hand but I'm hoping that just maybe… this one will be the one that re-writes history."

Raphael stood up, his black Templar uniform a stark contrast to the rest of surroundings, "You always talk of re-writing, Alcarde, but you never explain as to what you are trying to change."

Slowly the wizened old man rose to stand and ran his fingers through Fiero's dark hair, "A story which should have been written down correctly from the start. If this does not work… the last chapter will fall onto the hearts of the young who may not even know the truth of the matter."

Silence passed between the pair before a gust of icy wind ruffled their clothes and slightly dislodged Alcarde's hood. Wizened hands caught the material briefly and a chuckle, deep and rumbling came up from somewhere in his gut, "Looks like the old girl still has life in her. Come, we can't linger too long here."

Nodding, the younger vampire followed his lord and master but passed no comment worthy of note. Though he felt the bitter sting in his heart of regret and fear unlike anything that he had felt before.

The snow continued to fall silently, as it always did, but tonight the silence was much more noticeable. It was almost as if there should have been leaves falling swiftly down from the long, twisted branches that offered little to no protection from the biting wind. An interesting muse, Mephistopheles thought as he stepped down from the carriage he had been riding in to survey the scene. He held no love for this road, nor did anyone in the company with whom he currently travelled, but he knew that his insane mother would have her eyes very much focused on this area and he had to let her know that he was returning triumphantly.

A dry smile crackled to the surface as his dark eyes caught sight of his hand. The skin was starting to stretch, becoming almost paper-thin and see-through. A reminder that until the blood of the other flowed fully in his veins, he was not complete. Casting his eyes around the group, the vampire discounted the ghouls and human servants; he wanted living blood that was fresh and untouched. “Zarl,” he snapped towards a ghoul who was trying to look like he wasn’t lingering around too much, “There is a township near here, is it still inhabited?”

The ghoul blinked. “It was a trading place for slaves.” His accent was thick and rough, clearly beginning to lose the ability to speak after so many years of cruel unlife. “But the trade was stopped a long time ago. There may still be some illegal trades going on. What would you prefer me to fetch for you?”

Mephistopheles paused, glancing up at the sky in thought but his pale grey eyes picked up a little movement in the darkened shadows just off the path. “Bring me something pretty and fair. Bring a rat for Siren to stop that little minx from whining too much when she eventually awakes.” The ghoul nodded and bowed, before no longer being where he had been before. A dark glare was sent to the shadows and, for a millisecond, Mephistopheles thought of attacking but then declined. “What use are you if you don’t try to make him attack me?” A smirk crossed his features as he turned and nimbly leapt back across to the coach that he had been travelling in.

Ducking under the canvas covering, Mephistopheles felt a frown cross his fine features as he knelt next to an old-fashioned-looking coffin hewn together roughly by a bad carpenter. The man’s fear had been joyous to behold and it had been too much fun to sit and watch him. But that thought was pushed aside as the wax-like hand stretched out to lift the lid on the coffin and stare at the occupant beneath. The girl looked to be barely out of her teens, with luxurious pale skin and shimmering black hair. Her amber eyes, now closed in sleep, had been so full of life that the vampire wanted initially to tear them out with his own fingernails, but, in this enforced sleep, she looked more like a porcelain doll that had been safely wrapped away in cotton wool in the darkest attic.

Silently fingers stretched out to touch the fine skin, wondering what memories lingered as she slept. He took note of her finer features, the white wolf ears that were silk to the touch and the silver swirls on her body that were more prominent now. What could this creature possibly contain that was so vital to his mother? He had heard the stories of course, he knew the tale all too well, but he had to wonder why she just didn't take the destruction and leave the creation to whatever it wanted to do. Then another thought struck him, one that he had never considered before, "You, destruction? You are but a pathetic child…"

"One that managed to wound you and nearly kill your sister," a new voice said from behind him and Mephistopheles turned sharply, dropping the lid on the coffin as he did so and snarling at the grey-skinned mercenary with a greasy hair who now stood in front of him.

"Who are you and what are you doing here?"

The man smiled. "I am Jaru, Second Captain of Cresta Du Winters's personal guard. She sent me ahead to wait for your appearance and to gather information." There was a condescending tone to him, an arrogance that Mephistopheles hated straight away as no one had the right to treat him like a child. "My Lady bade me to return with news, but I can see that not all has gone to plan."

That knowing smirk was really beginning to annoy the vampire and the pale grey eyes glared at the almost incomplete creation in front of him. "Tell her that we are making good time and that we shall be back as directed. The Silver Maiden is secured and the guardian is long dead."

"Really now?" Jaru said, his voice dripping with the lower levels of sarcasm, which was surprising for a gargoyle, but he had heard that some were gifted with at least a little level of intelligence. "Is that why you are being followed?"

Before Mephistopheles could reply, a blade had lightly pressed against the gargoyle's back. Siren smiled wickedly at her brother. "Shall I cut out his kidneys or his spleen for us to feast upon?"

Mephistopheles smirked towards Jaru. "Appears that you have inadvertently awoken my sister, who is very hungry at the moment. I suggest that you leave right now, Jaru, and tell my mother that we shall be at the Manor within the next day if the pass is not blocked off with snow and ice."

Pulling away from the blade, Jaru seethed with anger before taking the moment to leave. The thump of him hitting the ground brought a giggle of delight from Siren who pulled back the blade. "Aww, didn't get play with the naughty man."

Appearing not to hear the other, the elder brother glanced down at the coffin below him. "Siren?"

"Yes?"

"Go hunt."

"Him?"

The vampire nodded. "Yes."

"He is mother's toy." Siren's words were laced with maturity for once; even though she was clinically insane, there were moments when her true age shone through, especially when it had to deal with Cresta's personal effects. "She will not be pleased."

"She won't even notice that he's missing," Mephistopheles replied. "Go have some fun."

For a second there was the slightest whiff of distain from the red haired girl but then a grin crossed her face and she glided out into the snow strewn darkness without so much as a glance back.

Another smirk crossed Mephistopheles's face. "Oh, if only all siblings were so easy to control. At least you, my dear disgusting half-sister, have the instinct to survive. It may be the only thing that saves you in the end."

The carriage rocked slightly as it went over a snow-covered stone. Mephistopheles Du Winter stared up at the canvas above him, wondering how much the girl in the coffin would fight to protect her life. He hoped it would be a good fight because it would be all the more satisfying to kill her and claim the powers for himself. A chuckle escaped him. "To think, the power of creation would be mine and I would be able to make it so that I was rightfully Mephistopheles from the start of time itself," he thought.

Chapter 9

Past Memories of a Time Not Mine

Dymas was well aware that he was dreaming as he stumbled, half-blind, across a vast desert plain which was literally strewn with bodies. There were humans, vampires, werewolves, changelings, witches, warlocks and a whole host of other creatures. They must have been battling for days, if not weeks, for there to be so many bodies and what disturbed him the most was that there was virtually no distinction between the different races. There were uniforms and clan colours but they were all intermixed and he noted that many wore the same colours. He didn't even know where he was going; just that he had to be somewhere. Somewhere in the middle of this field of death, but it was impossible to tell where that was.

Even the landscape gave next to no clue as to where he was; it was a featureless place, dotted with a few hills, but the sky was a murky grey and the clouds too distant to really be focused upon. There were no towers, no castles and barely any trees. It was an empty place, somewhere that had always been like this, or at least that was the impression that he got, but on the surface it appeared to have no immediate military advantage.

“Maybe it’s a source of magic,” he mused humourlessly to himself, staring around at the bodies which were becoming mere background noise. It was harsh, even Dymas understood that, but if this dream was supposed to be telling him anything right now it was that there was a lot of death to be had in war.

Something which he unfortunately already knew about, despite never having actually witnessed a battle of any remarkable numbers. Gently he shook his head, “If this is your work, old man, I’m not interested in going through any of your…” his words stopped when he suddenly found himself at the edge of a very large cliff that looked down onto an ocean that should have been roaring back and forth along the shoreline, but instead almost timidly lapped at the sand as if it were frightened to even make noise. The volf blinked his amber eyes, feeling the slightest of slight sea breezes and inner instinct told him to go down to the shoreline.

At the bottom of the path, there was a glimmer of sunlight through the clouds. It fell upon a figure who lay on her back, her black hair matted with blood and her pale skin virtually cut to ribbons. Dymas felt his stomach drop out of his body as a crow fluttered down from up above and started pecking at her glass-like, amber eyes.

“Ekata?” he whispered in horror, stepping closer to the figure and noting the other details that were so reminiscent of his twin sister. The wolf ears were present, though they were a heavy grey colour and curiously her fangs were extended down, looking like mock inserts that didn’t quite fit inside her mouth.

However, there was something different about the girl, the features were slightly off and, whilst she was clearly a young lady who had been virtually cut to pieces, something didn't fit right inside his head.

"Wait, who are you?" He took another step towards the girl. "Why do I know you… you are not my twin."

"Karlia!" A voice roared from above, causing Dymas to look up in total panic. "Karlia! Where are you?" There was a figure at the top of the cliff, just visible in the blinding light that was streaming through, but he was gone from view almost as soon as his amber eyes had latched onto him.

Dymas carefully turned back to the figure on the beach, noting that her blood was sinking straight into the sand rather than drifting out across it. "Karlia?" he questioned aloud.

"No!" The voice from before was suddenly right behind him and, before Dymas could move, a large man, donned in black robes and sporting jet-black wolf ears pushed quite literally through him to reach the stricken figure. "No! By the gods, please, no… Karlia! Karlia… wake up, you have to live, you have to survive this. Please, my little sister… please."

Blinking his amber eyes, Dymas stared at the man with a confused look. He felt cold, almost as if the grave had touched him, but, strangely, he also felt like he knew the other but couldn't place him in the slightest.

The man slumped to his knees and pulled the lifeless girl into his chest. "No! How could this have happened? Where is your guardian… why? Why did it have to be you?"

For a few long moments the man continued on with his ranting and ravings, screaming almost incessantly at the dead body which was highly worrying in the Volf's eyes as he was pretty sure that no one was supposed to really do that sort of thing. Vaguely he had to wonder just what he was being shown or where these strange thoughts had come from as they certainly made no sense to him in the slightest.

The crunch of rocks under sand alerted him to the presence of another and Dymas turned swiftly only to feel his heart clench. Tyra was standing before him, but instincts told him that this spirit wasn't the one who had mercilessly captured his heart all of those years ago. This Tyra was older and bore a choker which, the volf presumed, must have bound her to this level of reality. There was a sense of age about her, it sat heavy upon the broad shoulders and the hair was slicked back into a smooth style whereas his Tyra tended to look like she had been dragged through a hedge backwards several times over, even when she had tried to make herself look just a little bit more on the smart side.

The spirit's eyes flickered briefly over to Dymas, a look of confusion settling and the volf stepped back unsure if he were being really seen or not by the other. However the spirit, dressed in a fine royal guard armour, simply brushed him aside and took a step towards the black-clad man, "Deamal, we must leave this place soon. The tides of fate are against us and anything could wash up."

"I'm not leaving her alone like this, Tynan!" the man shot back, glaring over his shoulder to the spirit and shrugging the gently placed hand away. "She didn't deserve this fate. She was supposed to be…"

"Fate is cruel," Tynan said, kneeling down next to Deamal, "There was nothing that we could have done. She would have left our side even if…" gently the spirit sighed again and shook her head, "I know you hoped for more but she is what she is…

there is nothing that could change that. You have to let her go, right now, before it is too late for the pair of you."

Deamal looked down at the figure in his arms, at the tattered body and the dead eyes. Why did fate have to play this cruel trick, why did it have to always make those who were most innocent be so consumed by hatred and loathing? Why did the fates always target someone who had so much potential? Slowly he lowered the girl down to the sands, his black ears dropping in defeat and self-hatred. Dymas felt his heart clench again, the horrid thought of having to do such a thing to his own twin almost enough to completely wrench his gut out of his lower body.

He tried to picture Ekata, lying there in that beautiful white dress from the painting in the realm that his Tyra had created for him, to see her lying there dead and broken. A shudder went through his entire body, cold dread filling him as it felt so wrong and horrible. "Ekata," he murmured out loud, "please don't succumb to the darkness, you have to remain light."

Looking up, Dymas startled back when he found a pair of amber eyes boring into his own and found that Deamal was curiously staring at him. He felt like he was looking into a mirror, the face was recognizable and familiar but clearly not his own. "What are you doing there, boy?" the voice was quiet, curious and soft, more questioning as if he were just as confused as the volf was.

Dymas blinked, "I do not know…" It was a pretty poor excuse for an answer, even he knew that. "I found myself here."

"You are like me," Deamal stated rather than asked, barely aware that Tynan had knelt down next to Karlia. "Wait… I remember now. You are me."

"What?" Dymas had at least the sense to be a bit offended by the remark. "I am not. I am Dymas… and I am a Volf."

Deamal grinned cheekily. "Half-vampire, half-werewolf… with a younger sister?"

"Twin." The answer was short and snappy; Dymas was not one hundred per cent comfortable in this radically changing situation.

"Twins?" The word was whispered. "Is that what is missing?" Deamal glanced briefly towards the figures of his sister and Tynan, before turning back to Dymas. "Where is your sister?"

Dymas blinked slowly, feeling his insides crawl with discomfort, "Being brought back to the Manor so that Mother can try and remove the power that supposedly lingers in the pair of us together on our eighteenth birthday…" He glanced down. "Well, our proper eighteen birthday."

"Proper?" Deamal asked, frowning in confusion.

"We were born on 29th February, on a leap year. Even though we have lived a long time, the records say it is this year that we turn eighteen." Dymas wondered why he was telling the other these things which he barely spoke about to anyone, not even Tyra got this much information out of him.

Deamal paused as if in thought, but Dymas noted that he was staring directly at him in deep thought. "You have golden swirls upon your body?"

"Yes."

"Does she have silver ones?"

"I don't know." He thought it was best to answer truthfully in this situation, regardless of how strange it all was. "I haven't seen her in a long time. She was able to escape one night and meant to come back but…"

Deamal nodded. "Then you have given me some hope in my darkness."

"How?" Dymas felt as though he was getting a headache from this whole conversation. "Who the hell are you?"

"I am Deamal, the gold prince of creation, but I am half-werewolf… just like my sister." He smiled at the question which was clearly coming from the other. "Silver kills werewolves and if used correctly can seriously wound vampires. Gold represents the sun and it brings forth a new world whenever it rises. Gold is creation, deadly to us unless we embrace the truth of it."

Dymas blinked. "I'm creation?"

"Not yet, but you may be, or you may be the missing link for all of us." A gentle smile was directed his way. "When did you last see your sister?"

Dymas paused. "I don't know… forty years maybe?"

Deamal nodded. "More than enough time."

"For what?"

"Your mother, has she tried to remove your powers?"

"Plenty of times," Dymas said, rubbing his arms slightly and wondering when this game of twenty questions was going to end. "She always fails, though."

"Because you are meant to be destruction, right?" Before Dymas could answer, Deamal turned back around to Tynan and sighed. "Perform the rite."

The spirit looked up shocked. "What?"

"Don't let her pass over, you need to perform the rite and ritual… you need to do it now!"

"Deamal, have you gone insane?" Tynan stared at the black-haired male with a look that certainly said he was insane before her eyes flickered over to Dymas. "What did I miss?" Deamal smiled, "Nothing for you to worry about yet, my love, you need to do the ritual now else everything will be lost."

"But that means that I lose you," the spirit looked genuinely hurt by that statement and seemed to stare down into the sand with a well of sadness in her eyes.

Deamal carefully took the spirit's face in his hand. "But you gain so much more… take a closer look at that boy, Tynan. See what I can't, see what I had to learn through pointless questions… then perform the rite and end this terror that has been caused by me and my sister. Give us life anew… hopefully a better one that this."

For a second the male volf was about to interject with the comment that so far this life looked a whole lot better than his existence, but suddenly found those electric blue eyes on his and felt that rush of emotions which always ran through his heart whenever they got the chance. The gaze that held him was strong and powerful and he knew that it was probing every last detail and memory within him. Dymas let the spirit have full access, finding memories surfacing that brought on more memories. He was especially pleased when the images of his and Tyra's times together as one came to mind and lingered around far longer than the others.

Suddenly though, Dymas found himself unable to trust the spirit and he blocked her outright with a half growl. "Prove that you are her," he said, not quite understanding his need to know such a thing, but something deep in his heart told him it was for the best.

Tynan looked just a little put out by the remark and, for a second, he thought that he saw Deamal break into laughter as he pulled the body of his dead sister closer to his chest. Then the spirit in the royal guard armour stepped forward and placed her hand lovingly on his cheek, which caused beautiful shivers to go through his body.

Tynan smiled and began to recite an ancient poem, which Dymas was sure he had never really heard before and yet his soul knew the words perfectly:

"Malum non est necessarium quod a te
Multi enim dicunt quod malum ex vobis procreentur
Scio quod non sit intentio mala
Sed nec fuerunt nec erunt.

Vos diriguntur fata multorum
Habita atque adorati di ludos ludere periculosum tesseris
Tamen esse illum suum aliquando devolvunt
Deditque in illa die nemo dubitaverit
eventus

Non estis in interitum
Non estis monstrum
Tu quod mundus non videret
Nam id quod est vere est
Cor tuum, et percute me in aeternum
ut cum unus materiem

Iusiurandum sculptum creationem temporis
irrefragabiles
Mortiferum quasi lilium
Speciosæ sicut sanguis
Simul invenies viam
Princeps
Amica mea."

Dymas slowly opened his eyes after the words finished, and he stared with a small smile forming as he saw Tynan viciously lock lips with Deamal, much to the other's surprise.

"You had better not disappoint… Dymas."

A cheeky smirk came way too easily to his face. "You know I won't… Tyra."

There was a sudden blinding multicoloured light and, with a pained yell, Dymas found himself back in the burnt-out room with the figure in the black robe looming over him. His breath was coming out in short, sharp bursts and he glared up towards the man. "Let Tyra out, let us go!"

“I can’t do that just yet.” The voice was soft spoken, but held an edge which was not meant to be messed with. “But take it to heart what was said.”

Dymas growled, bearing his fangs which had dropped. “I am creation and she is destruction? That makes no sense! What the hell is the point of a woman being destruction… she should be creation.”

“Exactly,” the figure stepped back. “It may help you to understand some things in the future.”

“Wait! Shal!” Dymas yelled, completely forgetting where he was right now. “Why don’t you help us?”

“It is not my duty to, though I wish it was.”

The volf snorted as the shadow creature slipped away; clearly Shal was about to be found and there was next to no way that he was going to be caught around here once again.

However, a lingering thought crept into the volf’s head: “But remember, I am always watching and I will return my debt to you at the appointed time.”

Chapter 10

Lying to Oneself

The wind trickled through the cracks in the glass, almost as if it were probing rather than actively trying to pass through the once solid panes. It made an odd sort of whistling noise which was highly pleasing to the ear, almost as if a bunch of lost spirits were whistling instead of howling, and Cresta wondered just what tune they were trying to sing for her. For there was no one else within the expanse of the great hall, so who else could they whistling for? At times of clarity, Cresta Du Winter was very much aware that she wasn't entirely all there and could more than likely pinpoint the exact moment when her entire world had been destroyed, but those moments were fleeting. Especially when she was so close to gaining what she had been seeking for so long.

The power of creation and destruction, the abilities unmatched anywhere in the entire world. Soon they would be hers to wield and she would be ordained as an immortal living goddess who had control of the entire world. The puny humans would probably try to resist for a while, as they inevitably did, but they would make good sport for her fellow brethren as the new order was established and enforced throughout the world. The humans would fall, their power diminished in the face of the original children born from the ever dark and beautiful Lilith, and the werewolves would fall back into their original position of servants that were loyal to their vampire masters until death.

None of them would dare to even dream of touching a vampire lady's body, even in her direst of needs, and they certainly wouldn't try to steal the disgusting offspring that were born into the world, ensuring that they could grow up not knowing fear. It had been a stupid notion all of those years ago, and certainly wouldn't be permitted to ever happen again. Though if Cresta was truthful, she did rather miss having that *wolf* around the place. Maybe killing him had been a rather silly thing to do, she mused to herself, even if he had just been locked away in one of the darkest dungeons; at least there would have been something to amuse herself with, in between the numerous failed attempts to extract the power from the boy. Still Cresta shook her head, this time they would be successful and everything would be as it should have been.

A pity that she had been too consumed with accursed maternal instincts when those two brats had been born, it would have been easier to steal the powers before she became too attached to them. Not that she was attached of course; just unfortunately the curse of being a woman was a natural instinct to protect those small and defenseless things that had come out of her body.

"Well, that will all change for the better soon," she mused aloud to herself, staring around the room and almost twirling around in the multi-layered silk blue dress that she wore currently, "I will be free to do as I please and everything will go as planned."

For a second she waited for a response, waited for someone to try and oppose her or else propose a different version of events, but then remembered that she was the only one in this room as she had sent the servants away so that she could start the preparations for the ritual. She let out a satisfied smirk and nodded to no one. "As it should be."

Turning around, the vampire lady headed away from the grand ballroom and snapped her fingers at a group of rather pathetic looking slaves. "Clean this place so that it shines like starlight. Do a good job and I may reward you."

Not one of the slaves believed that they would be rewarded of course but they all bowed extremely low and scampered off to start their work. She allowed herself a thin smirk of pleasure before turning her emerald green eyes onto another figure who had materialized from the corridor. "What are you doing here, Akira? I sent you to track on the progress of Mephistopheles and the Maiden."

Panting heavily, the younger vampire stared levelly at his mother, as if he was trying to decide just how to best answer her. "I was. I am here to report back, Mother."

"So soon?" She sounded incredulous, almost as if not believing that Akira could have managed such a feat in such a small space of time.

The youngest son looked a little concerned for half a fraction of a second, but then gently shifted his foot down to the floor as he had apparently flown into the open window. Since this was on one of the top floors, this was a feat that was both impressive and unique, although it did leave him exhausted. Out of all his siblings, Akira had the unusual talent of being able to naturally shape-shift into a few different beasts. One of his favourites was to become a bat, as it allowed him the grace and silent movement to scan for many different sneaking operations. However, flying straight up a wall to a specific location still took a lot of energy and it quite frequently drained him.

At least Akira had had the time to pull on a pair of trousers before his mother had turned up, having kept stashes of clothes around the Manor for as long as he remembered. "I left two nights ago, Mother, I have only returned to you now."

Cresta blinked once again, seeming to glance at the clock with no real sense of interest before refocusing on the youngest vampire. "And what have you to report?"

For a fraction of another second, Akira wondered if this was the sort of response that her beloved Mephistopheles would have gotten in this situation, but then reminded himself that mother and son were far too much alike to really bother each other. Sometimes he really detested the way that she favoured the not quite eldest child, how she would lord him over everyone else as if they were nothing of interest to her and wonder vaguely how it had all come to this. What had he and his sister done to deserve such indifference?

However, Akira then remembered that in the grand stretches of reality, Cresta wasn't exactly fully of sound mind at the best of time and the woman who had been his mother was buried deep within her. "He makes good progress, they were close to the Byron Pass when I left."

"Excellent," Cresta smiled, turning to leave. "That means they should be here no later than tomorrow night. Perfect timing. I do so hope that the Prince will be completely prepared by then."

“There is something else,” Akira started slowly, but naturally pausing when a hand was flicked in his direction and the age old vampire in front of him turned with a slight tut. Clearly she wasn’t in the mood to hear anything else, but there was no way that he was going to leave everything unsaid in a situation like this. “Mother, please here me out.”

Cresta glowered at the other. “When did I give you permission to call me that?”

Akira chose to ignore her. “There are others following the progress of the Maiden.”

“As to be expected.” The woman didn’t sound at all fazed by such a notion. “She will inevitably gain interest wherever she goes.”

“But these are Hunters, dressed in the black garb which you warned me about on numerous occasions,” Akira said, stepping closer to the woman and desperately wanting to shake her. “They’re only a small number, but—”

A level stare that could have turned ice to water met his dark eyes and he felt a very cold and real stab of fear go through his chest.

“Why didn’t you deal with them, Akira?”

The male vampire gently chewed upon his lip. “One bore the symbol of Ak-Har on his neck…”

It was almost possible to hear the shattering of some inner glass phial inside of Cresta. The woman curled inwards on herself, shuddering and shaking her head. “No, not that is impossible! No such person exists.”

“Believe me, I saw it with my own eyes, Mother.” Akira sounded half-desperate; even though there were times when he wanted to grab the crazy she-devil by the throat and strangle all of the life force out of her, the woman was still his mother and, despite all of the evil things that he knew she had done to him and all his siblings, he still believed that the woman who used to smile at him gently every sunset and then sing him to sleep at the approach of dawn was still somehow there. That she could still be reached. It was the only hope he clung to, his only reason for remaining by her side. He wasn't strong like his real eldest brother, he didn't possess his sister's abilities to entice and confuse, nor did he have anything remarkably special about him like the twins did.

All he had was a very small glimmer of hope that his mother was really there, hidden behind the layers of the witch she turned into and that, one day, he would somehow bring about her return to them. Even if it was just a fleeting moment before she passed, Akira would see it even though he already knew that if it were a choice between saving her and saving the twins, he would always choose the latter first.

"I'll let you see if you so wish; if I prove to be wrong, then you can punish me." He offered his hand, knowing that Cresta could peer into memories so she'd be able to see what he was saying.

Cresta rose with a yell and slapped the boy across the face hard with nails drawn. "Don't say such things. You can't even remember what that mark looked like! How dare you say such things to me! Be gone from my sight before I turn you into dust!"

Akira didn't hesitate, hating himself all the more and turning abruptly away, planning on heading for the farthest point in the castle away from this crazy, raging monster. He hadn't made it two steps before light fingers grabbed onto his arm and held him back.

"Akira." The voice was soft and gentle now, so like the one that she used to use. "I'm sorry. Please… please come back, come back to me… son?"

Despite knowing that it was futile to even believe that Cresta cared for him, Akira still turned around. "I am willing to show you, though," he whispered, feeling the fright and hurt still lingering in his heart, "if that's what it takes for you to believe me."

"Shhh," the woman said, stroking the side of his face. "You don't need to. I understand. Go and feast on one of the virgins down below, Akira; regain your strength. We are all going to need it over the next few days. I am sorry that I struck you."

Staring at the woman for a few long seconds, Akira knew that his thoughts about the missing woman were true even if only for a fleeting moment. Silently he nodded, placing a light kiss on her forehead before stepping away quietly. Cresta wouldn't follow him or say another word and it was best to just walk away and take the moment as a brief, shining brightness that it was.

Listening to the sounds of the others footsteps fade away, Cresta blinked before turning her now steely gaze onto the open window and made to move towards it. "Who are you who dares to bear that symbol so openly near my home?" she wondered aloud, allowing her senses to roam to try and find the inevitable black spot. "You should know to leave well enough alone."

She was more than irritated when no response came and, after several more goes of searching, the vampire bared her fangs in frustration. “How, how is this possible? If it is you, then what are you trying to do by taking so stupid a risk?”

In a rage the vampire lady turned and stalked down the long corridors, trying not to give into the desire to just allow her memories to wander. She struck out, growling wildly and a suit of armour crumpled to the floor. Cresta barely registered it, all she could hear was the laughter of years gone by, the joy of her skin as those hands gently caressed her and the moments that they had only shared and it infuriated her beyond all of her limits. Cresta wanted to tear the place apart, banish those memories to the farthest recesses of her mind and never look upon them.

It was only the faint sound of water trickling over the rocks that made the vampire become aware that she had reached the fast-flowing river which ran along one edge of the castle and slipped away far into the night. The thoughts abruptly stopped as she stared at the water, which reflected back the black night sky and the distant stars. “If you lived, why did you leave me? Why did you abandon me? Force me to do that hideous act?”

“Hideous act?” A deeper voice spoke from behind, causing the woman to turn with a snarl, only to be presented with near impenetrable shadows. “Is that what you call it now?”

“Stop it,” she snapped at the shadows. “You are most definitely dead and the dead do not talk.”

Vaguely aware of someone brushing past her shoulders and back, Cresta shuddered.

A man’s voice chuckled deeply. “Yet here we stand, two undead vampires in conversation.”The bitter sting of tears was almost too hard to ignore but somehow she managed it. "I am not the dead that you are."

"Are you completely sure about that?" the voice was soft and warm next to her ear, gently caressing the skin in a way that only *he* had ever been able to fully do to her, "I've watched you from afar for so long and you know what I see?"

"A vampire," Cresta said, her voice devoid of emotion and filled with the true tone of her age. "A creature of darkness."

There was a single hum of a chuckle. "No. You're more than that, Cresta. You're a mother on the verge of breaking down; you're a child who's become lost to the world by her own choice."

"There's no way back for me." The words were still hollow. "I need that power, once I have it everything will be the way that it is supposed to be."

"Even you know in your heart that such things would never happen like that." The voice faded slightly. "You should try opening it once again. You may surprise yourself, my beautiful lady."

Sharp fingernails extended and Cresta spun around, slashing at the darkness but finding nothing there. Words tried to form on her lips, insults to be screeched into the night but they all faded on her tongue. "My heart beats for no one anymore," she whispered in defeat before staring at the roaring waters, "Not even the memory of you is enough to start it again." With a final glance to the swirling mass below, the vampire lady turned back towards her home, her mind clear and sharp. She would never be so weak ever again.

Chapter 11

Broken Glass

Aware that her abilities to remain within this level of reality were fading, Tyra had taken some time to try and sleep, at least so she could replenish herself upon wakening. But even managing the simplest of tasks proved difficult and the hours became long and drawn out. It appeared that Cresta had wised up to her ways and abilities, which was no real surprise though it was annoying. Gently she sighed, shaking her head as she pushed herself up from the floor of the jar. “Come on, you lazy old git, you can’t let him down now.”

It would have been easy to just switch off and return to the spirit realms, to rest and recuperate there and regain her powers properly, but that would mean leaving the love of her life alone and undefended which was something that the spirit just couldn’t do. Plus, time had a habit of passing strangely in the other realms. Sometimes she would be there for what felt like an age, but in reality only transpired to be a few seconds, whilst at others she would pop in to check something and step out only to find that years had gone by. There were very few spirits who could honestly manage to keep in contact with the living realm in such a constant manner as Tyra did and, for the most part, the spirit understood why most were content to remain in the deeper levels of the astral plains. It was quieter, more refined and so easy to control.

But Tyra rather enjoyed the madness of the living realm, how the different peoples moved through it and how it was always completely unpredictable as to what curve ball it was going to throw next. Quite a strange scenario to be in, really, but one that the spirit craved most of the time. Unfortunately, right now, she wanted nothing more than to have the simple options in life and, as she staggered forward to the glass wall in front of her, bare feet scraping against the marks from her earlier attempts to escape, Tyra couldn't help but feel like she was letting the volf down.

Though she was aware that the image was distorted by the powerful binding magics used to create it, Tyra knew in her heart that despite his bravado and snappy responses, Dymas was slowly giving into despair. This whole situation was getting more out of hand with each passing moment and, with the possibility of his sister returning, that despair was preying on him more and more. It was eating away at him, making him weaker than he had been upon the loss of his twin all of those years ago.

Gently she sighed, leaning her head against the freezing surface. "I will come and release you, Dymas, I'm not going to give up so easily." Pulling back away, the spirit stared up at the nearly impossible task before her and took a deep breath to focus herself for another assault on the walls of the jar.

To say that she was surprised when the floor beneath her suddenly lurched forwards wasn't quite the correct terminology. Her fingers clawed uselessly at the smooth surface as the jar haphazardly tumbled from one place to another and then back again. It was like being trapped in some form of very surreal dream and what was worse was that the jar kept on moving back and forth, changing direction suddenly as if being thrown around in a wide, erratic wind that made no sense and followed no established pattern. Tyra didn't even have the chance to yell aloud as the pressure inside the jar built up to an extraordinarily level, and then there was nothing but a blinding white light as the glass shattered in a variety of rainbow colours that tinkled down to the ground.

Slowly the electric blue eyes blinked quizzically open, bringing the dark room into focus as she stared around. Shards of lethal-looking glass littered the space, some merely resting where they landed whilst others were slammed into the wooden floorboards and walls at deadly angles that would slice the skin and spill forth fresh blood. The spirit felt herself fade for a few seconds, her instinct to return to the spirit realm in order to fully replenish herself having to be quenched. Focusing instead beyond that feeling, she realized that she was no longer in the room where Dymas had been; in fact, she was nearly at the opposite side of the Manor, which probably explained all of the strange movement which she had just been thrown into.

Still desperately ignoring her instincts to return to the planes, Tyra turned in a tight circle, focusing with all her deepest and darkest intentions to remain firmly in this level of reality. "Isa?" Tyra asked, shocked as she found the half-angel lying on his side in a broken, bloodied heap. Hurriedly, she rushed to his side and gently placed his head on her lap. "What did you do?" she asked in barely a whisper.

A sickly smile crossed the other's face, distorted by the wasted muscles and the taut skin. Tyra placed her fingers lightly onto the wounds and realized that they were far too deep and most certainly life threatening. Gently she shook her head. "I would have got out of there myself."

"It wasn't a spirit keeper," Isa said slowly, his voice cracking with the effort, "It was a…" A few long breaths escaped the boy, followed by a series of bloody coughs. "It was a destroyer. By the time you may have escaped, you would have had no physical form to return to."

"Spirit destroyers don't exist anymore; they were banished years ago…" Tyra started before looking down at her arms and realizing that she could virtually see directly through them. No wonder she wanted to return to the spirit realm to replenish herself, if this much damage had been done to her. Blue eyes moved up to the nearly dead black ones of the half-angel as she realized the sheer magnitude of what the other had done in order to get her out. "No, Isa, please tell me you didn't."

The smile turned sad, a slow and deliberate nod replacing the words that should have been spoken, "Like I said before, you are his guardian and he will die without you. My heart belongs to him but I do not… this way, I know you can help him… can free him."

"Don't you know the hell you'll end up in for breaking a spirit destroyer jar?" Tyra said, feeling her heart break and shatter at the very notion of just what could possibly happen to the fallen angel.

There came a smirking laugh, laced with blood and more coughs that ripped apart the boy's throat. "I doubt that it can be any worse than the hell that I've lived through for all these years."

Just looking at the boy, Tyra knew what he meant. His body was abused, his wings torn to shreds and any new feathers were pulled out by their roots in order to be used in the apothecary without a care. The bruises and impossible cuts on his face were clear indications that he had not lived a pleasant life in the slightest. How he was still able to smile was beyond Tyra's comprehension, but the spirit also knew that there was something that she could do.

"Then you shall not live through another hell," Tyra said, quickly placing her hands upon either side of the creature's face. The spirit ignored any stuttered cries that came her way and closed her eyes. Normally she wouldn't even need to pause to think before traversing the pathways of life and death but, being so weak, she knew that one wrong step could change everything that she had ever worked for and reduce her to nothing but a speck of imaginary dust.

It wasn't surprising that the Grim Reaper was extraordinarily close right now, but it did make her highly concerned that the bargain to save the creature's soul was easier than she thought it would. Maybe the old skeleton had cracked or gone around the twist, she wasn't sure, but it was something that the spirit opted not to worry about right at this second and sealed the deal before there was any chance of a change of mind.

Opening her eyes back in the realm of reality, Tyra smiled at seeing the look of absolute peace on the fallen angel's face as he finally passed over into the next life. "Live in joyous harmony for a while before you return," she said quietly. "May your next life be one of pleasure and joy untold."

Rising, the spirit turned and gauged her bearings for a few seconds before setting off at a quick pace. She had to get to Dymas and get him out of the castle within the next few hours. If she didn't manage that, then she didn't want to think of the consequences. It only took a few minutes for the spirit to rush through the corridors, slipping by gargoyles on guard duty and Akira who had paused only momentarily with a large book in his hands, but the spirit did not take note of the fact that he was looking out of the window.

Instead she hurried back to the burnt-out room and could only let out a small sigh of relief when she found Dymas was resting in the exact same place where she had left him.

The ghostly touch of a hand on his face made Dymas believe that he was still in the land of bitter dreams that were filled with nothing but regret once again. He had lost track of time, of where he was and what was happening to him. The male volf had simply wandered around in his head, bitter thoughts turning into agonizing memories of regrets and displeasures, of the times he wanted nothing more than to be dead and out of this hellhole that he called a life. How, when times became really bad, that he wished it had been himself who had been freed on that night all those years ago, how he hadn't given his sister a push at just the right moment to save her rather than have both of them be recaptured.

Thankfully however there was still just enough of a tiny spark inside his head that berated him for thinking that way. Whilst he wanted his sister to be in his arms just to know that she was alive, there was no way that he would have permitted her to go through the tortures that he had gone through. He would fight to protect her, would live to ensure that she became what she was supposed to be and nothing was going to stop him from achieving that goal in the slightest. The ghostly hand moved a fraction across his skin, gentle and caressing as if trying to wake him, but Dymas wasn't in the mood to play.

However the taste of soft lips, far softer than they should be but highly recognizable, on his own awoke the volf without so much as a pause and amber eyes found themselves looking longingly into the electric blue that were almost long forgotten. "Tyra?" he spoke quietly, not quite wanting to believe what he was seeing right now. "Prove yourself."

He wouldn't ask the cliché question because he had been fooled one too many times before. Whilst there were no two spirits alike, there were a few who could make themselves appear to be others and Cresta had tried in the past to use such tricks before. One time it had worked and the results were so terrible that Dymas was always extra careful whenever he awoke from some torture to find Tyra waiting for him.

The spirit smiled and, upon seeing that determined look in the other's eyes and feeling just a little bit more reckless than usual, she nodded. "As you decree."

Without warning, Tyra lowered her hands to the boy's waist and placed her lips on Dymas's exposed chest, just above where she knew the boy's beating heart would be, before taking a small teasing bite at the dirt-covered flesh with her teeth. The response was immediate, a breathy gasp escaping the boy as a whine of unexpected pleasure. "Tyra!"

The spirit had no idea what was so enticing to the other about having his chest bitten, but it was the one thing that she knew that only she could do to the other. Maybe it was just the rush of teeth being so dangerously close to his beating heart that meant the difference between life and death for the volf or, as Tyra liked to think, it was a very stark reminder of their first time together when she had wanted to do nothing but ravage the then rather young boy. Tyra had never been overly proud of what she had done to the lad all those years ago, despite her vast change of opinion from then to now, but sometimes she wondered if Dymas hadn't secretly tried to goad her into doing what she had done to him that night.

The volf liked things rough and needy, almost desperate and wild beyond the edge of what most could take, but Tyra always knew when to stop, when to haul the other back from the brink of that insanity and when to treat him gently and with love. Realizing that she had actually drawn blood, the spirit moved to close the wound, but Dymas mewled, "Drink from me, you need your strength back."

"I can live a lot longer that you can without strength," Tyra said, trying not to give into that temptation. "Plus we do not have the time. I need to get you away from here as quickly as possible." The spirit moved upwards, ignoring the wound for now as she would seal it closed once Dymas was no longer in his strange position of being chained up like this.

Thankfully the chains were not constrained with their usual hideous and deforming charms that caused harsh blisters and disgusting welts on the boy's skin. Tyra paused for a fraction of a second, wondering why Cresta would forget something which she used at any moment without so much as a thought, but presumed that it must have been something to do with the proximity to the 29th of the month. That made her pause again as she released the boy's arms. How close were they to that date? She had completely lost track. No wonder she wanted to get moving on her plan.

"Tyra," the boy whined, more demanding this time. "Please?" His arms fell down harshly, but he made no move to remove the trickle of blood which was slowly heading down towards his navel.

How she desperately wanted to say no to the boy, to tell him that she would give him every last ounce of his dreams and passions later when they were free and safe from the mad clutches of the insane mother of a vampire who wanted nothing more to destroy him and his sister. But when Dymas used that tone on her, virtually all of her self-restraint was taken away. She shuddered, "Dymas," she made the mistake of looking up into the boy's face.

The next thing either volf or spirit knew, the boy's legs were freed and they were on the old burnt-out bed, the last few scraps of clothing removed with ever hurrying movements. Tyra latched onto her previous mark, running her tongue along the full path the blood trail had taken and loving the sounds that came from the volf as she did so. "We shouldn't do this," the spirit said, pausing briefly to look up at Dymas.

The amber eyes were sparkling lightly. "I know… but are you really going to stop?"

Their lips crushed together, bodies entwining, and they both took what they needed from the other. Neither questioned how come no guards tried to enter the room or how this whole situation seemed to be masked from the rest of the household.

The pair just expressed their needs, wants and desires for each other in the only physical way that they knew how.

Shal, the Xian, shifted into a more naturalistic looking shape just outside the door and made sure that the barriers, which he had put in place, were still functioning. He knew that he was playing a very dangerous game right now, but he knew that they would both need something to cling onto when the moon finally finished its climb up into the night sky. Blood would be drawn tonight, and not the type asked for in the heat of passion.

Chapter 12

Blood Moon Waning

Carefully Tyra poked her head outside of the room, letting her senses roam. Something was strange about the night air that much she could tell, but for the life of her it was impossible to pinpoint what was the cause. Part of her instinctively tried to retreat back into the room, to return to her spent lover on the old collapsed bed and remain there, but the spirit wasn't about to let this opportunity slip away from them. Without a sound she became ethereal, moving swiftly down the darkened corridors and through the ancient stonework to obtain the materials that she wanted.

Concern grew in the spirit's heart as she made her way through the building, virtually unopposed by anything expect the odd slightly startled mouse who scurried away. It felt like she was moving through a thin layer of thick treacle, but it was even affecting the other realms of reality which felt as though something was slowly trying to choke her.

She found what she was looking for in a sealed trunk in an unused bedroom. The clothes were probably a little bit on the big side for the male volf but there wasn't the time to be picky. Unlocking the door, as she couldn't make physical objects pass through into the ethereal realm which allowed her to traverse through things, unlike taking someone's living conscious to a separate realm which was well within her abilities, Tyra headed as swiftly as she could down the corridor and into the stagnant air.

She headed straight back to the fire-burnt room, noting that the affects of whatever phenomena was happening right in the outside world were not as noticeable in here, but those thoughts stopped when she spotted Dymas over by the window, his white hair blowing as if in a breeze.

Something immediately spiked within her, warning of a great danger. Since there was only one other supernatural creature who was apparently walking right now, Tyra knew that it was coming from the volf. "Dymas?" she asked carefully, slowly, keeping her voice neutral though she didn't quite know as to why.

There was an extraordinarily long pause before the male turned to look at her with blazing red eyes. Gone were the soft, familiar features and the almost hopeful glimmer to the amber that she was used to. Standing before Tyra was something that intended only one thing, to hunt, to kill and unfortunately for the spirit, it had just found a worthwhile target.

Dymas let out a sudden growl and spun on the spot, a sickening crunching sound as bones and flesh virtually tore themselves to shreds as he changed to a creature of dark black fur, muscle and piercing white teeth that extended far further than the usual wolf's. Long black claws, the colour of midnight managed to just gain a grip on the destroyed wooden floor, tearing up chunks as the beast charged straight towards

Tyra in a mad frenzy of gnashing teeth and unmistakable growls.

Strangely Tyra didn't feel any fear, at least none that showed as she smirked wickedly. It had been an awful long time since she had felt the thrill of the hunt and whilst she was the provisional target, the spirit knew all too well that she could use this well to her advantage. Nimbly she dodged aside from the hulking creature which smashed through the door behind her and out into the corridor beyond. "Come and chase me, big boy," the spirit laughed gleefully, before taking off at breakneck speed down the corridor with the monstrosity tearing after her.

Tyra led the creature on a merry dance throughout the halls, just remaining out of reach at all times but always just aware that one wrong move and Dymas would be devouring her. Well attempting to devour her, though if truth be told Tyra didn't actually know what would happen if the other really did get his teeth into her flesh. She knew that she could escape from werewolf and vampire alike, that was simply a case of delving back into the deeper realms and remaining still for a long time, but a volf? They operated on a completely different scale and whilst she knew that Dymas couldn't willingly traverse the separate layers of reality, in this mad and angry form there was no telling what the other may be capable of.

Not that these thoughts were anywhere near the spirit's head naturally as she ran through the mansion, allowing the creature to stumble and crash into walls and objects in a mad frenzied dash. Whilst she didn't want to harm her lover underneath this monster, the spirit was hoping that at the very least some of the defensive charms could be broken by the creature. There were sparks of power flying off the fine fur and the glow to the red eyes suggested that there was magic within the boy that was being fuelled by this rage.

When the spirit nimbly ducked a pounce, causing Dymas to go straight into a large pillar, there was a flash of dark blue which scorched the floor to literal cinders in a matter of seconds and produced a stench so vile that it made Tyra feel sick. The blue eyes slowly raised back to the creature, watching with a fascinated horror as it pulled itself up from the rubble of the pillar with purple, black and the odd green orb of light bouncing off the dark fur with next to no affect.

The blood-red eyes glowed brighter and the growl that came out of the monster suggested something had changed. It was only then that the spirit was able to just briefly focus beyond the creature, out into the open courtyard where the sky hung like a thick and heavy blanket. The moon was blazing in the space above them, a blood-red moon that nearly sucked all the air from the spirit's physical body. Its rays were just grazing the tips of the raised hackles on the volf in front of her and Tyra knew that now she had to get them both out of harm's way.

If Cresta found out about this, she didn't want to think what that crazy vampire would do to them. Slowly she rose, never taking her eyes off the creature in front of her which only slightly shifted in challenge and she nodded. "I understand, I must be quick to avoid you now," Tyra said. "But I know your still there, Dymas; I will bring you back from the brink."

The monster was suddenly on her, far quicker than Tyra had ever dared to believe that the other could move and the spirit uncharacteristically yelled as the sharp teeth snapped at her face. Her hands gripped at the rough fur, clinging to the ears and pushing back for all of her worth. “Dymas!” she yelled. “I know you’re there, come back to the light! I will not hurt you or abandon you!”

A paw clawed around her chest, ripping through flesh to cause long trickles of black blood to leak from the now open wounds. For a briefest of brief seconds, the spirit saw that the paw changed back to the more normal human appearance when it scrabbled at the broken flesh and ran over the spirit’s blood. Looking up at the monster, Tyra suddenly knew what she had to do. How she could save her enraged lover despite the fact that it would destroy Dymas.

Vampires needed to drink blood, werewolves needed to eat living meat and bones.

With a roar Tyra pushed the monster off herself and started running again, leaving an easy-to-follow trail as she headed away from the Manor, as the scorched floor had caused one of the wooden doors to turn into ash. Tyra led Dymas through the courtyard and down a blur of corridors which led to rooms that had not been used for centuries. They were suddenly out in the large garden towards the back, a place which had at one time been beautiful and a welcome retreat from the stresses of the night but now it was an abandoned place where roots overgrew and ivy choked any wild flowers that tried to push through the undergrowth. The only flowers that still remained where the stunning white and yellow dove petal ones which the twins had accidentally called forth one day. Cresta had tried multiple times to have them removed, but each and every time they had just returned.

Instinctively, Tyra grabbed two of those flowers as she leapt over the small hillock and ripped them out by the roots, one white and one yellow. She was beginning to stumble, her breath becoming ragged and she knew that soon she would end up in a whole load of trouble which would not be good in the slightest. If she could just get to the cliff edge beyond the trees there was a chance. The monster was virtually breathing down her neck now and the hot odour filled her nostrils as the creature took a bite… but just missed.

That was way too close for the spirit's liking and she forced herself to move faster, knowing that she wasn't far now. She was almost surprised when she cut through the trees and suddenly found herself on the precipice of the cliffs staring down at a roaring waterfall. However, before she could even begin to properly think through this crazy plan, the monster that was Dymas had pounced on her from behind and the momentum sent them both tumbling over the edge and into the fast-flowing river below. Water engulfed her form but the spirit didn't care, she was more concerned with stealing her own subconscious away from her physical body as the claws and the teeth buried themselves into the prey despite the fast-flowing waters.

Tyra knew that this crazy creature would have no troubles in finding a safe passage out of the water, but if she lingered in the physical body then her life would be ended. Just as the strong and powerful jaws found purchase and snapped her neck, the spirit ripped herself away to the darkest parts of the spirit realms and lay there panting in fear and relief. Briefly she glanced back, watching as the monstrous wolf stalked onto the shoreline and started to devour her former body. "Do not despair Dymas," she said quietly to him. "When you awake, I will be back by your side."

Finally, the harsh feeling of being trapped lifted and allowed Cresta Du Winter to pull herself slowly up, away from the corner. Just what was that strangeness that made her want to hide away and never come out? She was a vampire, one of the most feared creatures in the entire world; there was nothing that should have been able to terrify her so much that she wouldn't move. Curiosity got the better of her and she stepped to her door, opening it just a crack and feeling the slight emptiness of the house. Even the servants had hidden from the terrible feeling.

A frown crossed her features as she made her way carefully through the wrecked corridor, wondering what could have possibly caused it. "What monster has been through my home?" she snapped at the nearest other living thing, which was unfortunately a mouse that scurried away as fast as its little legs would carry it. She stormed angrily towards the nearest window, determined to drag her poor excuse for a son out of his sorry existence when, just out of the corner of her eye, she spotted the moon. Normally she would ignore it as it was just a large lump of rock in the sky, but tonight she felt inexplicably drawn to it.

"It was blood red before," Akira's voice cut in from the side; the younger vampire was huddled in an alcove, looking terrible. "The whole surface is covered. I've never seen something so terrifying."

A kindness overtook Cresta, her youngest child looked distressed beyond anything but yet he had weathered the horror by staring at it. Maybe there was something more to the youngest vampire than even she knew but, right now, her deeply buried mothering instincts were brimming up to the surface and she couldn't willingly neglect him. "You stared at it the whole time?" she asked, kneeling close by and wondering why he backed away from her for just a few seconds.

Akira nodded. "From the moment it started to change... it was just a normal moon, like thousands that have been up in the sky before but then the red came, boiling out from the centre as if something had been woken and was spreading. It felt so cold, so wrong and filled with an evil that I haven't felt since..." he stopped, not wanting to utter another word and looked down.

"Since when, my son?" Cresta asked, reaching to touch his hair as gently as he could.

The younger vampire shuddered. "Since the day the twins were born..." His voice was so quiet that Cresta barely caught the words, but she blinked at him and glanced back at the moon. A thought had stirred within her head but it was one that she wasn't entirely sure about. She thought back to when she had first heard of the birth of the maiden and prince, how it was supposed to be a glorious occasion where a great calm came over everything. But thinking back on that day, there had been nothing of the calm. The twins had been premature and for a while it appeared that the vampire lady had miscarried because there was so much blood.

Out of instinct she had birthed the babies, rather than risk getting cut open only to find them covered in a black slime which surely meant they had passed on in the womb and her heart broke into a million pieces. Whilst she hated what she had done against the memory of her beloved husband, she was still a mother and her instincts had been strong. She had cried for the twins and reached for them, pulling them close and away from the clinging blackness so that at least they could have a moment of bliss. Her tears had hit them and their bodies were stiff as they were stillborn.

Then the blackness had evaporated from the pair, it had almost appeared to wither away and suddenly the boy started screaming and moving, slowly awakening his sister who took longer to start crying and Cresta had been terrified. It was strange realizing that was the point where she had become scared of her own two children but, now that she was thinking clearly, it was also the moment when she had just about given up on them ever existing.

She blinked down at Akira, whom she was holding and thought back to the day that he was born as well as his older sister and brothers. What had changed on that day when the twins had come into existence, why had she gone from despairing for their loss to being mortally terrified of them to the point where she rejected them? Her eyes flickered back to the moon, narrowing a little.

Something else was playing games here, something that she didn't think that she could deal with.

Chapter 13

A Gift from the Grim Reaper

Slowly coming to his senses, Dymas blinked and stared at his hands which were covered with a milky black blood which he was sure that he had seen a few times, but couldn't quite place as to where he had seen it before. His amber eyes blinked repeatedly, fighting off the feeling of fatigue and a gnawing sense of horror. Though he had no real idea as to why until he focused beyond his hands and felt the harsh bite of the cold wind against his bare skin. A body lay not too far away from him, though more correctly it should have been described as a carcass. Someone had been torn to shreds and pretty much every last piece that was edible had been devoured.

"No... Please, no..." Dymas shuddered and looked down at himself. "Please, tell me no..."

He was covered in black blood, his bare body barely showing any signs of wounds received and for the first time in as long as he cared to remember, he felt no trace of the lingering hunger which would plague him on a daily basis. There was only one culprit to the crime in front of him, but he had no memory of what had happened in the slightest.

His eyes roamed over the wreckage, looking for some sign or indication of which poor wretch he had destroyed before he spotted a crop of blonde hair. Horror turned to terror and then to despair as he pulled the fine strands to himself and was struck by the scent. It was Tyra's carcass in front of him.

"No!" he screamed. "Please! Wake me up, I didn't mean for this! Please, please."

How he wanted this to be another illusion to try and draw forth his power, how he wanted this to be nothing more than a nightmare because he had destroyed his lover, something which he never wanted to do.

He wailed to the night, hearing his mournful howls echoing back at him and eventually came to the realization that he was awake this time. Dymas wept bitterly, damning himself to every last level of hell and hating himself all the more. How could he have done this? How could he protect his sister if he went and did this to his lover? He was useless and disgusting, just as his mother had said over all the years. Vaguely he was aware that he had puked up whatever remained of Tyra in his stomach and for hours he lingered in the darkest shadows, hiding from the moon. As the sun began to peek over the horizon, the volf made a decision and despite the tears that were still falling from his face, he set about with the task of dealing with the remains.

Lovingly, he gathered them together in a pile and surrounded the remains with rocks and a few branches, those which were the least snow-covered. Kneeling next to the mound, Dymas hung his head in shame. "I'm sorry, Tyra, I didn't mean for you to go through that ...I hope in another life... you find someone better than me to love."

Slowly, he extended his hands over the mound and the gold swirls on his body began to glow bright before a soft golden light moved down to the remains. Closing his eyes, Dymas wept harder and just let the heat of the flames that arose from the burning corpse lick at his skin.

He could feel the sun creeping higher in the sky behind him, the bare skin on his back quickly beginning to blister but he wouldn't cry out in pain, not after what he had done. He didn't deserve to live after all of that and, despite the fact that he knew it would leave his sister with no further protection, at least his mother wouldn't be able to steal his godawful powers.

"Tyra... Tyra," he spoke aloud, sure that his end was nigh. "Come back to me. Come back now."

Without thinking, Dymas opened his eyes unaware that they were a glistening gold and felt a sudden shift in the air. Silver light poured out of his chest and expanded around him in an all-consuming way that made him believe he was finally being granted his wish to just die. Though just as the last piece of his broken and tortured conscience slipped away from him, the world returned to how it had been before, causing the volf to jump in surprise.

Instead of being the cold harsh winter, it was almost as if summer had visited the small bank side that he was on but it had quickly given away to autumn. There was the pleasant smell of horse chestnuts in the air and the breeze was warm and playful, causing the red and brown leaves to flutter down to the soft ground. There were glistening yellow flowers in the mound where Tyra's remains had been and, for the first time in a long while, he felt safe and secure.

He virtually jumped out of his skin when a warm brown cloak was placed around his shoulders by familiar hands and he spun on the spot to be greeted with those stunning blue eyes.

"As you commanded, my Prince," Tyra said with a smile, leaning forward and placing a kiss on the stunned boy's lips before he could say anything.

Dymas pulled back in horror, unable to believe what he was seeing, but then a searing pain went through his body and he yelled out. Tyra grabbed him tightly and held him, feeling the strange autumn around them suddenly burst and become the harsh and bitter winter. The only thing that the spirit did notice, however, was that her burial mound remained almost untouched by the snow and ice. The stunning yellow flowers shone out brightly in the dimmed, winter sun.

For a long while Dymas was out cold, seemingly dead to the world and Tyra used that to her advantage. She cleaned him of the blood and muck which had clung to his body for far too long and dressed him in the clothes that she had found in the Manor before all of this. There had been a cave not too far away from their position by the river bank and the spirit had moved them both into that area, hiding Dymas away from the scorching sunlight that still somehow managed to make the snow twinkle all around them. It was a beautiful sight to behold, one that was uncommon even for these lands, and the spirit remained faithfully by Dymas's side as he slept.

His chest rising and falling was the only indication that he was even alive right now, the spirit having to reach across every so often and confirm for herself that there was indeed breath coming out of his nose because she could not lose him now. Not after having gone through all of that, though if ever asked Tyra would never dream to describe the sensation in the slightest. It was one that could not easily be put into words and she would never have the heart to tell Dymas about it. She could only hope that he would awaken soon, else they would linger too long and that would only bring Cresta's gargoyles ever closer to their location.

Though as the sun began to rise on the second day of their being by the lake, Tyra found herself drawn outside of the cave where a figure stood in a long cloak. She blinked in the fading light and frowned, "You're not one of Cresta's little minions, I'd remember you."

The tall figure smiled, his black eyes gleaming with mischief, but he nodded. "You are right, my lady, I am not one of hers nor am I one of yours."

Tyra narrowed her eyes. "Then who are you and what do you want?"

"I'm here to check that our prince is fine," the figure said, taking a step forward before lightly raising his hands in surrender towards the fierce-looking priestess and sighing. "I am on your side and I have here a drink which shall help him to wake."

"You haven't given me your name and, since I don't know you, I'm naturally inclined to be very suspicious," Tyra snapped, annoyed that she couldn't get a usual astral spirit reading of him to learn the truth of his intentions without having to ask them.

The man smiled. "My name is Shal, and I am a Xian who serves a master who is keenly interested in seeing that both Ekata and Dymas survive."

The spirit tutted. "No wonder I can't get a reading on you. Though you've either just arrived here or have been useless in helping us out."

"On the contrary, I have merely kept my presence masked from yourself because it could have led to many troubles," the Xian continued, licking his lips lightly. "Dymas knows of my presence and I have frequently helped him in the darker times when you have not been available."

A nasty glare was sent his way which made the Xian chuckle aloud. "You are certainly the Golden Priestess of old," he said before shaking his head lightly, "I have never touched Dymas in any way other than to offer him kind words when he has been separated from you, my lady, and I believe that the precious gift you gave the fallen angel will be a turning point for all the sins that were ever allowed to be committed in the Mansion behind us."

That stopped Tyra from snapping at the Xian and she frowned a little. "So why only reveal yourself now?"

"Because their birthday grows closer and their powers are changing things without anyone noticing, bar myself and those who watch the streams of time," Shal replied, offering the bottle. "You have to try and get Dymas away from this place and the sooner you wake him up the sooner you can both be gone. I have confused the gargoyles with a barrier for the past day and I can keep it going for another, but if you linger too long they will figure out that something is wrong and come hunting for you."

Taking the bottle, Tyra pulled the top off and sniffed the contents, frowning when she found it was only water. "This won't help in the slightest," she said offering it back to the Xian, who stepped back away from her.

"It is the purest water from a fountain of myth that will ensure that Dymas lives," Shal spoke reverently. "He needs to see you alive and well, locked finally in this form so that you share your lives until the final breath."

"What?" Tyra asked, staring at the other in confusion as she was certainly not aware of anything like that.

Instead of responding, Shal merely raised his fingers to his bare neck and tapped it a few times. Tyra frowned towards him, but compulsively felt the urge to touch her own neck and found that there was a choker there that she had previously not noticed. Rushing to the water's edge she stared at her reflection and found that it was a black choker, with no clasp to undo it with and a golden pendant set with a blood-red stone that would not yield to her fingers' gentle exploration.

For a moment she blinked, trying to think of when she had made such a deal with the devil before remembering the pact that she had made to allow Isa to pass into a better life.

Offer your Immortality for the boy and he shall live his next life in pure joy and happiness with a mother and father who will care for him forever.

"I am mortal?" she spoke as she rose to her feet, confusion rippling at her brain.

"But with all your abilities from before," Shal said from the opposite side of the river, a hand raised in a cheeky wave. "He did not take your most vital assets as he knows you have to fight long and hard next to your prince, but do not think that you are unkillable. The ancient rules still apply and too much exposure to one thing will certainly kill you."

About to argue, Tyra let out a groan as Shal slipped away to his own devices and she huffed before looking down at the bottle in her fingers. Could this small slither of water really wake Dymas up and get him moving again? She would wait until the sun set to try it and prayed that whatever gift had been granted did not come with a price attached to it. Though the thought of being completely mortal did not shock Tyra as much as it meant that, one day, once her lover was free from everything, then she would be able to give him what he wanted.

A family of his own, to love and cherish beyond all other outcomes.

Chapter 14

Bringing Forth the Gold

The snow was probably still the same stuff as what had been lingering around for the past week, but to Dymas instead of feeling cold and unforgiving on his bare feet, tonight it somehow felt soft. He felt like he was walking on air, despite the fact that he was still bitterly weeping for what he had done and was basically allowing Tyra to pull him on through the barely visible path. The spirit had initially been carrying him, but the volf had demanded to be set down so that he could walk himself. It was the only thing that was stopping him from breaking down, as he knew that they had to keep on going.

Part of him knew that they had tried this route many times before, that it was watched, and that they should try to get somewhere safer and more off the road, but he was just so confused right now. He had killed his lover, brutally ripped her to pieces and devoured everything, but somehow the spirit was here, leading him away from the Manor which had been his torture ground for so long and, in his mind it just wasn't possible. Even if somehow the spirit had returned to the realms and healed, there should at least be a long delay in doing so.

He pulled himself up short, causing the spirit to stop. "Who are you?"

Tyra sighed a little, but not out of frustration. She understood her lover's anxiety and confusion over this whole situation and knew that there was still some of the werewolf preying at his mind. Whilst the moon had returned to its normal colouring, there was still a small red dot which indicated that the red moon would rise again, and Tyra wanted to be as far away from the Manor as they could be before that happened.

"I am yours, my prince," she said, gently pulling the other into her body, "I am Tyra, even though I know it is hard for you to accept."

Dymas moved to pull away, "But I killed you... her... the original spirit! I devoured her and burnt her remains. I am truly destruction..."

Without uttering a word, the spirit pulled the volf into a hug, holding him tightly despite the boy's physical protests at such a thing. "No, you're not. Not yet," Tyra spoke calmly. "My heart still beats, you can hear it and feel it within you. I promise you that this is no trick and no deception. You brought me back to you and I still love you with all of my heart."

"How?" Dymas half-wailed. "How is it even possible? You once told me that if you lost your physical body then it could take years for you to return. You were barely gone a day... I had to... to..."

Quickly Tyra placed her lips on the panicking boys, letting him feel and share in the warmth of their shared feelings for each other. She knew that the other was scared, confused and hurt by everything that had happened but she also knew exactly how to deal with a troubled Dymas. Their lips moulded together and their tongues danced, the taste the same as it always had been, as were the tingles of pleasure went throughout their whole bodies.

Slowly they parted a soft smile on Tyra's lips. "I will explain everything once we are far away and safe, Dymas, but know that I am truly yours as I have always been and I will not allow anything to hurt you ever again."

There was a sudden twang and they looked up to see an arrow lodged in the rocks just above their heads. Tyra wasted no time in grabbing tight hold of the volf and started running despite the pain which would be plaguing the smaller male right now. The barrier that Shal had used must have dissipated and the gargoyles were clearly hot on their heels. More arrows whistled overhead, some just nicking at their clothes and one skimming across Dymas's cheek to draw blood as Tyra paused briefly to get her bearings.

Ducking into another pathway, Tyra pulled the shaking volf under the cover of a worn-out and very unstable-looking wooden bridge. It was not the best hiding place in the entire world, even Tyra acknowledge that, but hopefully with the gargoyles' inbuilt fear of water they wouldn't dare to try to come anywhere nearer the pair. Granted the river was partially frozen over but there were occasional trickles of water which would undoubtedly keep the gargoyles at bay lest they be reduced to their component parts.

"Spread out," a voice that was deep and gruff shouted and for a second Tyra did not recognize it. That was until the wooden boards above her creaked and the fully grounded spirit looked up. There was a gap just large enough for her to see a gargoyle who was tall with thicker-looking pebbled skin and a mouth shaped like that of a dog rather than the beak they usually possessed. He bore a plumage of black feathers tinged occasionally with white and the spirit could not help but let out a silent gasp of surprise.

Malino was the gargoyle that Brutus had created, spending hours crafting him out of a rock which had tumbled down from the mountainside and he was his second in command. Fiercely loyal and unknowing of fear, he was literally only a few steps behind Brutus in terms of strength and capability. "Search every last place they could be, including under the bridge or else I'll rip you to pieces and throw your remains to the water to devour."

Tyra stared down at the male volf who was beginning to shake. "Are you okay, Dymas?" she whispered, barely making a sound.

Slowly the boy shook his head, blinking his still glowing golden eyes. "No… I feel…"

Tyra ran her long spindly fingers into the other's thick white hair, only mildly surprised to realize that she could find the boy's wolf ears far more easily than she normally could and sighed. "Don't think of it. I will get you out of here."

Turning his gaze up towards the other, Dymas took the moments of panic to really look at the spirit in front of him. She was tall, with wispy black hair and those same stunning electric blue eyes which had always enchanted him. The body beneath his fingers was firm and strong, muscled and built like that of a warrior, but twining around her neck was a choker. Blinking his eyes, Dymas thought back to that strange dream-like memory of the other spirit, and knew that for once he did not have to be scared of his powers.

"Tynan?" Dymas whispered gently. "Help me to release."

For a second the spirit looked completely lost as to what she had been asked and turned towards the boy with a frown. However, when their eyes locked, the spirit let out an all too familiar smirk. "Don't phrase it like that, it makes me think of other things."

Dymas smiled seductively back and ran his fingers teasingly down her stomach before lightly sticking his tongue out at his lover, for she could only be that. "You know what I'm like."

The spirit smirked back playfully for a few seconds before glancing up at the bridge above them as Malino presumably took a few brave steps onto the bridge to search the land for any signs that would expose where they were. Locking eyes with the determined volf in front of her, Tyra silently nodded in agreement.

Dymas smiled towards Tyra before slowly taking a deep breath and closing his eyes, grounding himself. He didn't entirely know what he was going to do or try to accomplish at this moment, but he knew that if they lingered here then they would be caught.

All thoughts left his head and he focused, searching for that one thing. The one thing which his mother had been desperate to get her hands on since she had realized just how potentially powerful both of them were. Dymas turned, still feeling the spirit at his back and extended his hands outwards in front of him with his palms up. "Eroz," he spoke aloud and immediately a new brightness began to flicker the markings on his skin. It pierced through the air, reaching to the ice below and causing it to creak and groan. A few seconds later it cracked and large sections tore away, slamming onto the unsuspecting creatures that pawed terrified at the edge of the river banks and sending them sprawling with a variety of screeches. Dymas didn't stop there though, the beams of light continued straight into the streaming water which was finally free of its enclosed prison.

Within seconds, the fast-flowing stream was steaming and bubbles of heat rushed to the surface. Malino howled and, in a move to prove his stupid fellows wrong, stuck his hand into the boiling mass and let out a horrendous cry which pierced through to the very soul.

Tyra grabbed tight hold of Dymas and whispered, "Time to go." Closing her eyes, she focused and felt the familiar white light surrounding them.

The next second they crashed onto the top of a frozen waterfall and both went skittering towards the edge. Dymas scrabbled at the ice, feeling small peels of his skin ripping away from his bare hands and body and knew that he had tumbled over the edge when he felt the air being stolen away from his lungs. Tyra was right besides him within seconds, grabbing onto his body as they tumbled towards what would only be their ultimate end. Though with a blaze his eyes glimmered golden and Dymas extended his hands upwards with a cry of, "Eldora! Visit this land!"

The ice gave way as the pair smashed into it but instead of the feeling the bitter cold, which would normally have ripped them to pieces, the volf was only aware of pleasant warmth which soothed the soul and brought back memories of those sweet and precious moments long forgotten. Instinct made him kick out when he felt the rocks below his feet and he knew that Tyra was still firmly by his side. Breaking the surface of the warm water with a held in breath, the volf panicked for a second when he went back underneath but was quickly hauled back upright by Tyra, whom he automatically clung to, breathing quickly and heavily.

"What, what just happened?" he asked, caught up between a thousand different emotions and wanting at least an answer which would make sense in the quickest possible way.

Tyra looked around the previously frozen and dark valley, blinking her strange eyes, "I think you brought back something."

Blinking, Dymas chanced a glance around himself and stared in awe and wonder.

What before had been a dark and unforgiving place with mean twisted rocks that tore at flesh and bone was now a lush valley in the hues of autumn after a long and joyful summer. He blinked gently at the surrounding land, noting that the trees were no longer gnarled and lost-looking, that the water flowed freely and more calmly now and that there was a distant scent in the air. One that reminded him of long nights spent huddled together for warmth, of gentle smiles and softly spoken promises and of someone whom he longed to see more than ever even though he was terrified that it may bring about nothing but doom.

Casting his amber eyes to the right, where a small embankment was, Dymas found himself more than a little disappointed when he did not see a small wicker basket and a familiar smiling face of a beautiful young woman with golden hair who was not his mother. He sighed, "Why did I bring this back? If I couldn't bring her."

"Don't think about it too hard, Dymas," Tyra said gently, heading towards the embankment as fast as she could manage through the softly flowing waters. "None of that was your fault, nor was it your sister's. It does no good to dwell on the past, I have come to learn."

"I thought that we were meant to learn from our mistakes," the male volf replied as he was set down on the surprisingly soft ground. "All I have done the last few days is kill and destroy without thinking of what I was doing."

Tyra sighed, placing her hands either side of Dymas's face to make the boy look at her. "Dymas, killing needlessly is something that you have not done. Not once in your life. You have been tricked into killing, tortured to the point of starvation and made to believe that you had no other choice. Today you had to kill those creatures because they would have devoured me and taken you back to that blasted monster of a woman who dares to call herself your mother." She took a deep breath. "What you did to me was not killing."

"I tore you apart and ate you," Dymas virtually wailed towards the spirit. "How is that not killing?"

"My blood is the only thing that can turn you back from being that monster and I am the only creature in the world who can survive it," Tyra replied, calmly and with a gentle sereneness to her voice. "Just like your sister, who can only drink from one truly in order to quench her thirst when the vampire takes her. It is one of our most sacred and secret duties as guardians."

Dymas blinked slowly at Tyra. "Did you know this?"

"Truthfully, no," Tyra said with a smile, lightly pressing her lips to the boy's. "But even if I had been aware of such an important duty, I wouldn't have turned my back on you. I've never done that, regardless of how many lives I've gone through with you, my prince, and I still love you regardless of what happens from now on."

"I don't deserve you," Dymas said slowly, wrapping himself close. "You're too good for me, Tyra."

The spirit chuckled, holding the volf tightly for a few seconds. "Correction, I'm possibly the worst thing that ever happened to you."

Another series of gentle kisses were placed against Dymas's lips, the spirit tempted to do more but instinctively knowing that it would not be a good idea right now. "Now, wait here a moment; I'm going to find you some food and then we are going to get out of this accursed valley and go and find your sister."

Chapter 15

Meeting Old Friends

Having been able to feed and dress Dymas in dry clothes, Tyra had made sure that he was really ready to move on before starting off down the path that would lead them down towards the valley. They had lingered for a better part of the night but the spirit wanted to be completely sure that they were not followed and that her prince had enough strength to carry on. Plus she did not know the full extent of the effect that the boy had caused, but if the pathway was as clear as this then they would make very good time. But suddenly she came to a stop and pulled Dymas tightly behind her.

"What's wrong?" Dymas asked, glancing around his guardian and seeing nothing for a few moments before a figure appeared at the top of an outcrop of rocks. He was a young man, rippling with muscles and jet-black hair that almost shimmered in the light, but that did not detract from the stunning silver eyes that sought out the pair which flashed in surprise and fright before something else filtered into them as he stood there, unmoving.

Two other figures were quick to appear, a man who looked like a vampire but was hunched over in a cloak clearly meant to disguise what he was, but there was a certain power behind him that made appearances clearly deceptive. Dymas found that he couldn't really focus on this figure for very long, instead finding his eyes landing straight onto the third figure. This was a much younger vampire, who wore a black Templar's uniform and who had long black hair tied back in a neat ponytail. He exuded a familiar warmth from his grey eyes, which immediately caused a gasp to escape from Dymas's throat.

"Mephi?" he whispered in surprise, not believing what he was seeing before launching himself towards the vampire to throw a tight hug around him. Raphael looked somewhat surprised for a second before returning the hug wholeheartedly.

Fiero glanced at the pair in confusion before turning his eyes back to the spirit, who looked just as shocked as he did. Oh well, at least they were together in that department, which was good. However, he took a few more seconds to blink at the spirit and felt memories returning to him, "Well met we are again Tyra."

Tyra looked a little offended for a second, staring at the unknown wolf before her own memories returned. She blinked. "Wow, Fiero, finally manned up, have we?"

"Nice to see you too," Fiero stated, shaking his head and then noting the spirit's determined glare towards the first vampire. "He's the reason we got here to help you, don't worry, he won't do anything to stop us."

Tyra glared towards Alcarde. "He better not, else I will rip him into a million different pieces and ensure that he cannot—"

"Tyra," Dymas spoke lowly, his amber eyes flicking to his lover in warning, "this is neither the time nor the place." His eyes flicked to the werewolf, realizing that he was the one whom he had seen in the painting. "Why aren't you trying to save my sister?"

Fiero glanced at the boy who had slightly disentangled himself from Raphael now and was glaring at him with anger burning brightly in his eyes. The werewolf sighed, "That's what I'm here to do, but at the same time we also need to save you. If we work together we stand more of a chance than if we are apart."

Alcarde nodded. "I like your thinking but we are going to have to move fast and I can't see how we are going to have that good of an opportunity to do much."

Raphael had glanced over the cliff edge and looked down, surveying the scene. "Whatever you've got planned, wolf, you're going to have to act upon it within the next few minutes before they pass through here. The roads are next to impossible to ambush from this point onwards."

Fiero nodded, glancing around the group. "I know that. Dymas, I know this is rude of ask but we will need your powers in order to save my mate and your sister."

Dymas blanched slightly in fright. "I doubt very much that I can help you. I barely know them myself."

"Dymas," Tyra said carefully, "you know them more than you have ever let on. Maybe not consciously but you have been using them for a great deal of time. Do you want to save your sister?"

"Yes, of course," Dymas said, not taking his amber eyes off the spirit in front of him, "but I don't know how to control them. What if what he asks is impossible for me to do?"

The spirit smiled slyly. "You brought this place back to its former glory and whether you want to admit it or not, you helped me to return to your side. You do not have to fear what you can do, Dymas, I am here to protect you and guide you. That flea-bitten ratbag over there is here for your sister. This is the one time where you can fully use your powers and regardless of what happens we will be there for you."

"Plus, you won't be the only one," Alcarde's voice came deeply from behind them as he indicated towards the top of the waterfall where a wolf made of white fire glistened above the raging waters, "I believe that is Jared?"

Fiero nodded. "Yes, Ekata called him forth upon his death to be remade anew. I didn't think he would follow us this far."

Staring at the creature, Dymas blinked and looked down at his hands, thinking about the last few hours. "She gave someone a new life," said the volf. He slowly blinked his eyes and let out a long drawn out breath. "Destruction and creation are one and the same, aren't they?"

Tyra looked towards Dymas with a slightly confused expression but then smiled and nodded towards the male volf, pressing a kiss to his forehead. "Yes, in order to create something, you need to destroy something first. In life for everyone that dies, a new life starts somewhere else in the world. That is the balance that always constantly has to be maintained."

The male volf nodded, looking towards his hands once again before he turned to look at Fiero, a new determination in his eyes. "What do you want me to do?"

The werewolf looked a little on the uneasy side for a few seconds, clearly choosing his words carefully as he knew one slip in his words could spell trouble for them all. "Get Ekata out of that coffin she is trapped in. The more you can make your presence known, the better for us."

"What?" Tyra sounded incredulous over the idea. "You want him to risk his life for you?"

Fiero shook his head. "No. Not in the slightest. Other than that accursed vampire below Dymas is probably the only other one who can break her out of that contraption. If that vampire is distracted, he won't think that an attack will come his way."

"You plan on double teaming him?" Raphael said carefully, trying not to sound like he was jumping the gun. "Or do you want to take your revenge on him?"

"Neither," Fiero said, shaking his head. "Mephistopheles will go for Dymas, regardless of whatever else is going on around him. He will be the distraction, is all."

"Then what are the rest of us going to be doing?" Tyra still sounded highly annoyed.

A smirk passed the werewolf's face as he slightly tilted his head to indicate Alcarde. "Waiting for him to make his move."

The creature blinked, clearly surprised by the turn of events and looking rather horrified, but then a slow realization came across the features and a wicked smile broke through the old form. "Your uncle told you something that he shouldn't have, didn't he?"

"Not in so many words," Fiero responded, "but I figured it out. There's only one vampire that my father would have ever dealt with on any level. Mephistopheles has faced all three of us and he knows how to battle us, how to defeat us. He probably even knows how to knock Dymas and Ekata about without really trying. *You* however, I very much doubt that he'll know anything about."

Alcarde smirked. "You're still playing a dangerous game, boy."

"Maybe, but it's a route that he won't expect us to take," Fiero smirked back, equally as wicked before turning back to the volf. "All you have to do is break the seal on the coffin and help your sister out but most of all you have to be seen to be doing it."

"What if Siren gets involved?" Dymas asked with a shudder. "She's quicker and more deadly."

Raphael coughed. "You don't need to worry about her. She's on our side."

Before another word could be spoken there was a sudden boom from behind and flames licked up into the air. There came muffled screams and shouts, followed by a blazing crack as more deadly flames trickled along the brittle dry wood of the carriages.

Fiero cursed. "Jared. Always had to make a scene."
Dymas however didn't hear him, having watched the white-flame wolf glide gracefully down from the top of the rocks they were on to charge through the carts and horses without appearing to need to wait for anyone but himself. The flames licked up brightly and smoke plunged up into the sky from the surrounding snow, but the volf knew there was no second

chance. Leaping off the small cliff, he ran half blind for the cart where he knew his sister to be, trying not to cough in the choking smoke that swirled around.

Followers screamed, lost and confused in the madness as terror gripped at their hearts and minds and somewhere he was sure that he could hear Siren wailing, but knew he had to ignore it for now and just keep on going. Even without his close connection to his sister, it was easy to find where she was as the coffin glowed with silver light.

He scrabbled up the wood, and grabbed with the lock and the seal. For a few seconds he didn't know what to do, the metal feeling hot in his fingers, but hearing the girl scream from within made him focus. "I'm coming, Ekata! Hold on!"

Dymas focused, his golden marks shining brightly and the lock cracked before crumbling away and the elder brother flung the wooden top off before reaching inside to pull his twin sister into a hug. For a second, he was aware of complete and total chaos all around them, and then a blinding light plunged everything into darkness.

Chapter 16

Choices to be Made

Slowly his senses began to return, though it felt as though he were waking up from a long, dark and very deep sleep. Images and sounds blurred together, incoherent and barely formed in his stumbling vision. The only thing that he was fully aware of was the fact that his feet were moving, that he was dragging someone. Dully he became aware of voices and sounds, distant and vague as if someone had placed cotton wool into his ears and then taped over them. Something gave way under his foot and he tumbled to the ground, and he felt nothing but heavy breaths escaping his chest. The air was so thick here, it was nearly impossible to breathe and part of him just wanted nothing more than to go back to the dark void.

However something shifted off his back, and he heard a sound that felt like something he hadn't heard in a long while. "Dymas?" the feminine voice asked in confusion before a half choked sob escaped. "Dymas!"

Something heavy hit against his arm, causing him to yelp slightly, but it wasn't in pain; it was more annoyance because the person had hit right on the spot that always jarred the funny bone. That was quite specific knowledge and the second strike to the same area brought the world back into focus, the dullness disappearing to be replaced by a sharp whistling noise before the final hit to the arm, which was harder than the others brought his senses snapping back to reality.

"You better wake up or else I'll…" There were the sounds of tears in the voice and Dymas turned his head sharply, blinking at seeing a beautiful young lady to his eyes. "Ekata?"

The female volf smiled with relief for a fraction of a second but then looked up sharply, ducked down to cover his frame as a piece of burning wood went whistling overhead and then clambered upright, dragging Dymas up. "We need to go! If we don't…"

A quick glance around the burning carriages, and the sounds of battle were more than enough to spur the male volf on without any further questions and they ran together, trying to head away from the wreckage. There came an odd sort of howl from behind them and Jared appeared, running ahead clearly leading them to what would hopefully be a safer place.

Just as they reached the edges of the fiery chaos, however, there was a roar of defiance and Mephistopheles appeared slap bang in front of them with a dangerous scowl on his face and a blood-red sword lined with black runes pointed straight at their throats.

"And where do you two bastards think you are going?" the enraged vampire snarled, raising the blade and taking a swipe at the pair of them, his eyes ablaze with the rush-wreck fear of fire that most vampires had.

Just unfortunately for the pair, it had chosen to manifest itself as rage. Ekata pulled Dymas back a step or two, but knew that at this moment they were pretty much cornered.

Especially when the blood-red sword cut through the flame wolf of Jared to dispel him back to the netherworld until he could be called for again.

"Mephistopheles!" the name was shouted by two strong voices and suddenly the two guardians appeared in front of the pair, their own weapons brandished and glowing.

"Let them go," Tyra said, her eyes a piercing blazing blue that shimmered out of the red fire as she swung the warhammer expertly around in her fingers. "This madness has to stop."

Fiero raised his sword defensively for a second. "You're outnumbered. You've lost half of your followers and if you think you're getting through us you are clearly just as insane as that mother of yours."

A snarl came in reply and suddenly the vampire was in-between the two guardians, slashing at the werewolf and kicking the spirit away with sharp moves and snarls that made the blood run cold. To keep the spirit occupied he threw a curse of swarming instincts at her whilst he full-on attacked the werewolf, knowing that he was the lesser of the two guardians with the misfortune of being born mortal. Whilst werewolves lived an extraordinarily long time, they were far easier to kill than most other supernatural creatures. "The day I bow down to filth like you, is the day that I die and that shall not be today!"

Metal collided with metal in a deadly dance, but then a hand clamped down onto his shoulder and a twisted grin crossed the face of the spirit as the swarming monstrosities, which had been trying to infest the spirit's body, instead charged to the living flesh of the vampire.

Mephistopheles howled in rage and both guardians took the opportunity to break rank and run towards their respective partners. Before either could reach them, a cage made of living tree roots sprang up around Ekata and Dymas, locking them in place.

Fiero managed to get an arm through one of the gaps to make a grab at Ekata. "We will get you out! Don't panic, my love."

"Watch out!" both twins yelled as Mephistopheles was suddenly back into the fray, looking angrier than before and Fiero was knocked to the side, the blade poised straight above his heart as if to slaughter him. Tyra acted fast, blocking the blade with her war hammer and locking it around, so that the sword twisted in the vampire's grip and then was sent skittering harmlessly out of reach.

"Back down," Tyra said, her voice laced with deadly intent, "and we may just let you live."

Mephistopheles chuckled wickedly. "When do I ever take advice from *servants*?" Flicking his wrists, long black tendrils of smoke latched onto the spirit and drove through her body, shimmering brightly in the fires dancing around them, and the spirit let out a wail of pain that came from her very soul.

Thrusting himself upright, Fiero charged once again at Mephistopheles, trying to bring his sword down onto the tendrils that held the other guardian only to find that the vampire used his other hand to make a new set latch onto him. The pain was the worst that he had ever experienced in his life and it took all of his strength to not yell out. There was no way that he was going to give the vampire the satisfaction of hearing him plead for his life.

“How does it feel to have your soul being ripped out, Guardian?” Mephistopheles laughed, certain of his victory and clearly getting drunk on the power that he was stealing. “How does it feel knowing that you are powerless to stop me?”

Suddenly the vampire blanched and let out his own wail of pain and discomfort, releasing his two prisoners and staggering backwards as plumes of red made their way down from holes that had inexplicably turned up on his body. His furious eyes glanced up, seeing his two bastard siblings standing facing one another, hands clasped together and concentrating. The faint glow of silver and gold around them was slowly dissolving the cage. He could only presume that they were reversing the effects of the spell he was using and an angry growl escaped his lips. Mephistopheles leapt upright, taking a charge at the pair, the blood-red sword nimbly called back to his fingertips.

Before the blade could strike though, another darker blade moved in to block the attack. “I would not advise such a move,” a rolling voice from the depths of the past spoke to him and the dark grey eyes turned in horror towards the owner, “I already spilt enough of this family’s blood a long time ago and I don’t particularly wish to do so again.”

Dark grey eyes widened in sudden shock upon seeing a large man, possibly reaching seven feet tall, towering over him with strong muscles, long black hair and blazing eyes which bore straight into the young vampire’s and brought to the surface memories that he had long ago thought suppressed and gone from his subconscious. “No,” he said, pulling back. “No… you cannot be here. You… you died!”

"Even after all your learning in the art of illusion, you still refuse to see what is before your very eyes?" Alcarde said with a smooth tone, shifting his stance a little and raising his blade. "You're making a grave mistake by even believing that you could steal their powers. I would have thought that I raised you better than that."

Mephistopheles snarled, "You barely raised me and don't talk to me as though I'm the worthless one here. You are the one who abandoned your family and allowed their wife to sleep with a servant to produce those disgusting creatures over there. Don't you dare speak to me like I'm the one who's worthless!"

"Angell," another voice spoke, bringing back harsh memories of darkness and another vampire stepped behind him, his long dark hair glistening in the roaring flames as Raphael stared down at his brother. "It doesn't have to end like this. We can help one another this time; make things right as they should be."

The vampire named Mephistopheles laughed, "You really think that I am going to back down now? After so long? You think that seeing two dead walkers would change my mind so much that I wouldn't change my plans after so long?"

"What is that you so desperately wish to change?" a new voice spoke, this time belonging to Ekata who was just behind her guardian, both slim hands wrapping gently around his arm. She looked so serene, despite being terrified, confused and clearly wanting to escape from all of this madness. Her amber eyes held a glow of love, but it wasn't just for the guardian who clearly had her heart; it was for something else and the vampire couldn't help but look towards her stomach.

Shouldn't there have been a wound there? Didn't he strike her through the middle? Taking a harder look at her, he realized exactly why he wanted to kill her outright there and then. Her eyes held the look of an expectant mother. She was with child and that infuriated him beyond anything that he could describe. How could something so disgusting and downright ugly be granted the ability to produce another life? His eyes flashed red and his fangs dropped. "You should have run bastard, instead of exposing your filthy little secret to me!"

He charged at the female volf again, managing to avoid the attacks that came his way from both Alcarde and Raphael and sent the werewolf reeling into the nearest burning cart. Raising his blade he went to strike at the girl only to find a golden vine wrapping around the blood-red steel and a surprising force of strength pulled him back. Dymas looked furious as anything, his amber eyes blazing.

"How dare you try and take her from me!" he screamed at his elder brother. "Over something that you threw away! Is this what all of this pain and torment has been about all of these years? Is that why we were subjected to torture and chaos, because you lost something which you wouldn't fight for?"

The vampire was surprised by the sudden edge of understanding to the younger voice, though instead of making him see that everything was justified it only served to make the volf more furious than before. Mephistopheles tried to pull himself out of the grip of the golden rope, as he was not going to lose his sword again in any battle, but instead was forced to let out a yelp of pain when a similar silver rope latched onto his arms and legs, effectively pinning him in place.

"Angell!" Raphael started again. "Your anger is misplaced. These two are not responsible for what happened to you or to me. They just had the misfortune to be born at a time when mother needed something else to blame."

"Boy," Alcarde spoke again, "you need to learn to let go of this mask you put up for yourself. You need to be your true self again if you are ever regain what you believe was taken from you."

Mephistopheles spat at Alcarde. "What would you know of such things?"

"Tyra," Alcarde spoke, his voice level and calm, "can you do what must be done?"

The spirit glared a little. "I am not leaving Dymas undefended. We are still too close to the lands for my liking and—"

"I can do it if you want." Siren now approached, a gentle blue glow of water on her fingers which doused the flames around her. "I know a fair few tricks of the mind."

"Siren?" Mephistopheles stared at the vampire lady who approached him, her head held high and barely a trace of the madness which she had succumbed to over the years present on her features. Instead of the ragged little girl whom he could order around with next to no hassle, the vampire saw the other for what she truly was. A vampire lady of old who knew her place and was fully in control. "How long have you been deceiving me?"

"Since the day I was born," the girl replied, stepping close and placing her hands on the side of his face, the gold and silver ropes disappearing to be replaced by the water ropes that latched onto his body far tighter. "Well, since the day I had my second birthing. It is now time for you to open your eyes and see the truth that has been hidden from you for so long."

Fiero and Tyra shared a quick glance and silent nod, carefully taking hold of their respective partners and moving away. Alcarde raised a silent eyebrow towards them but Raphael smiled and nodded, "We'll meet you at the pass. Hopefully with our other brother who is harmless as they come."

Tyra nodded. "Yes. The scholar boy… be mindful of him. He may be a fool but he is a smart one."

Raphael nodded and turned his attention back to the screams, which were coming out of Angell's mouth as Siren worked through his mind to virtually tear it apart, so the vampire could see just exactly what lies and double visions he had been through his entire life.

Chapter 17

Final Light

For a long while, the group of four walked in silence, no one speaking or feeling the need to do so. The night was dragging slowly to a close and the moon was beginning to set from its high position in the sky. Slowly and naturally Ekata came to a stop, allowing Fiero to continue on a few steps as he remained holding her hand, and she only smiled gently when he turned back to silently ask her if she were okay. Nodding she inclined her head towards her brother and the werewolf chuckled. "Five minutes and then we must continue on, my love."

"I understand," Ekata said, her eyes sparkling. "We won't be long."

Tyra rolled her eyes, pressing a kiss to Dymas's temple. "It'll give me a chance to talk to that scruff of a mutt of yours. Getting knocked about like a puppy, honestly, what sort of guardian does he think he is?" There was a teasing tone to the spirit and she moved quickly down the path to playfully harass the other guardian, but it was clear that it was all in just good fun.

For a few seconds the twins stood beside one another, aware that a few more steps would take them completely out of the lands that belonged to their mother and it would mean that they were safe and free of all that they had gone through for so long. Dymas turned to his sister at the same time as she did, happy to embrace her in a hug of genuine joy and hope. Their fingers intertwined in the middle, he using his left hand whilst she used her right. After all these long years of being apart, they were just on the brink of freedom, of being in perfect balance with one another and being able to do whatever they wanted with their lives.

"You know, don't you?" Ekata whispered, her breath slightly tickling his ear as she kept her voice out of the wind in case either of the squabbling guardians heard them.

Dymas paused, gently licking his lips. "Unfortunately so. Are you sure you can go through with this?"

"No," the girl replied honestly, "but we have no choice in the matter. If maybe a day or two could have been spared…"

Pulling back, Dymas lifted his sister's face with his free hand and smiled gently at her. "We both knew that it would never happen. That's the trouble with fate."

Ekata slowly nodded, smiling a little. "At least this time, we will be together."

"Yes," Dymas grinned, even though he knew that the darkness was approaching with every passing second, "and, this time, we have more of a reason to fight."

The girl blinked curiously at him and he almost chuckled before gently pressing his fingers to her stomach. "I want to see my nephews and nieces outside of a painting in a level of reality which is only controlled so much by me. This time we will change everything for the better."

Ekata stared at her twin and glanced towards the guardians who were beginning to playfully fight each other in good natured fun. "I wish we could tell them. Just one, you know."

"It doesn't work like that," Dymas sighed, looking down at Tyra and smiling. "It'll never work like that unless we put an end to it."

Instead of answering, Ekata turned her amber gaze up to the horizon, watching as the sun began to climb upwards, spreading the yellowy pink through the dark blues that still lingered. Several stars remained in the sky, as if beginning the marking of something extraordinary. Gently she sighed, closing her eyes, but never once leaving the tight grip of her hold on her brother. "Happy birthday, Dymas."

Dymas too glanced up but his eyes instead went to the moon which was just beginning to appear out of the last of the glowing embers of the sun. "Happy birthday, Ekata."

A violent screech ripped through the air and tumbling through the shadows of the forest came a boiling mass of grey smoke which sparked with black lightning. It engulfed the twins in the time it took them to turn their heads towards the sounds and suddenly the pair found themselves face to face with the woman who had given birth to them so long ago.

Cresta Du Winter's eyes blazed with triumph as she snatched hold of each of their arms. "Always said, if you want a job done, it is best to do it yourself. Say goodbye to your puny little lives and come with me to meet your real destiny!"

Within an instant the trio was gone and Tyra ran to the spot where the twins had stood, reaching it first ahead of Fiero and fell to her knees almost in total despair. "No, no, this cannot happen! How could we have been so blind?"

"I don't care," Fiero said, grabbing the spirit by her shirt and hauling her upright. "We go after them right now. There's only one place that they would be taken."

"And teleporting will be no good," Siren said, approaching the pair quickly. "There's already spells up to prevent that."

"We take to the valley in front, the river hasn't covered that land for years," Raphael said, staring up at the growing darkness with a sigh, "though Brutus will probably have his whole army out there waiting for us."

Both guardians nodded and, without asking further questions, ran straight towards the battle that they knew would be looming, flanked by Siren and Raphael who were already drawing forth their weapons in keen eagerness.

Alcarde turned to the other vampire, who looked diminished now and seemed to still be angry. "I won't ask you to choose sides as that is not fair. But think about what you know and make a choice with your heart and not your head, Angell."

With that, the creature disappeared from view, turning into a large vampire bat and taking off into the growing light. Mephistopheles remained on the ground for a few long seconds, before looking up at the dark building that was his home in the distance. Correction: that *had* been his home. He gripped the pommel of his blood sword. "My name… what is it worth now?"

"More than you know…" Another voice came into his hearing and the vampire turned, his eyes landing on the Xian. "… if you are prepared to let me show you."

For a second, the vampire thought about cutting the creature down. Instead, he extended his fingers out to the other and found himself oddly praying that, for the first time in his life, he was actually making a choice that was his own.

Latin Poem Translation

Evil does not need to be delivered from you
For many say that evil is born of you
I know that evil is not your intention
It never was and never shall it be.

You are guided by the fates of many
And the gods play dangerous games with dice
However I shall one day be the one to roll them
And on that day, no one will doubt
The result

You are not destruction
You are not a monster
You are something that the world should see
For what it truly is
Your heart and mine beat forever
As one

An oath carved in the creation of time
Unbreakable
Deadly as the rose
Beautiful as the blood
Together we will find the way
My Prince
My Love